MUTUAL
ADMIRATION
SOCIETY

"So you're Johnny Liddell?" Her green eyes hop-scotched approvingly from his broad shoulders to the rugged planes of his face. "Thanks for coming."

"I ran all the way," Liddell told her.

"Like a drink? I could sure use one," she said.

Liddell nodded and sat down on the couch. He watched with growing satisfaction what happened to the low neckline of her gown when she leaned over to splash some liquor into his glass.

"This means a lot to me—your coming here on such short notice. As I told you, my friend in Las Palmas will pay you ten thousand dollars to find the man who murdered his—uh—partner. My friend also said that the situation is so urgent that I'm not to let you out of my sight." She leaned over to pour another drink and Liddell gave up once and for all his battle to keep his eyes on her face. It was a fight he lost happily.

"There's a flight to Las Palmas in the morning," the redhead said. "I know you weren't counting on being cooped up with me here in this apartment all night. I'll try not to be too much trouble."

She wasn't.

DUE
OR DIE

FRANK KANE

First Fiction House Press Edition July 2018

Originallly published in 1961

isbn 978-1947964679

www.FictionHousePress.com

ONE

Larry Adams sat at his desk in the den of his rambling ranch house five miles off the Strip in Las Palmas. A desk lamp that spilled a triangle of white light down the list of figures he was studying left the rest of the big room in semi-darkness.

Adams scowled at the figures, picked up a pencil, did some rapid computing on the desk pad at his elbow. He rechecked his totals, looked impressed.

He was so engrossed with the figures that he didn't hear the French doors from the patio slowly open. A man stepped in, satisfied himself that the man in the chair was alone. He crossed to the back of the chair, leaned over and slipped his arm around Adams's neck in a murderous mugger's grip. He yanked the head against the back of the chair, tilted it toward the ceiling.

Adams struggled futilely, clawed at the arm that was cutting off his wind. His eyes rolled up to the face of the man leaning over him, widened as he recognized him. He redoubled his effort to break the grip.

The mugger reached into the side pocket of his jacket, brought out a knife. There was a faint click as the four-inch blade snapped into place.

Adams was struggling for breath, pleading with his eyes.

The man with the knife reached over, the knife sank home to the handle. Adams's body jerked spasmodically as the blade bit into him, lunged forward against the restraining arm, sagged back into the chair. The mugger withdrew the blade, plunged it into the dead man's chest a half dozen more times as insurance. Then, calmly, he wiped the blade off on the dead man's shirt, snapped it shut and returned it to his jacket pocket.

He relaxed his grip on Adams's throat, walked to the desk, picked up the figures the dead man had been studying. He tore the top sheet off the desk pad, checked the totals, whistled softly, stuck both sheets of paper in his pocket. While the killer looked around to make sure he had missed nothing, Larry Adams sat in his chair, legs stretched out in front of him, watching him with dead eyes. A thin red stream ran from the corner of his mouth, matching the dark red stain on the front of his white shirt.

The killer, finally satisfied that he had missed nothing, walked back to the French doors. He took a last look around to make sure he had left no traces, then he stepped out, carefully closing the doors behind him.

TWO

Johnny Liddell was sitting on a stool in Mike's Deadline Café, morosely studying his reflection in the backbar mirror. It didn't look any better than he felt. He dropped his eyes to his glass, found it was empty again, signaled for a refill.

Muggsy Kiely was in Hollywood on another screen writing assignment, and suddenly New York had lost most of its excitement for Johnny. He contemplated the feasibility of getting aboard a jet and surprising Muggsy in the morning.

The idea had two drawbacks. First, Muggsy's disposition wasn't of the best in the morning and she might not see the adventure in its right light. Second, some hasty mental arithmetic turned up the fact that he'd have difficulty financing a Long Island Railroad excursion to Montauk Point, let alone a flight to the Coast.

The bartender finished aiming one of his overdue commuters in the general direction of the door, shuffled down to Liddell. He saw the condition of the glass in front of him, made a production of selecting a bottle from the well. He filled the jigger to within a hairline of the top, slid it across the bar without spilling a drop.

Johnny Liddell has less success in transferring the

contents to his glass. The bartender grinned, leaned over and swabbed up the spilled liquor with a damp bar rag.

"Takes a steady hand," he commented.

Liddell nodded. "I don't live right."

The bartender scowled in the direction of the doorway. The overdue commuter had somehow gotten turned around and was heading back to the bar. The man behind the stick muttered under his breath, shook his head. He started toward the end of the bar.

"Stop being such a killjoy," Liddell grunted. "Let the guy live a little."

"I'm not worried about him," the bartender flung back. "But his old lady threatened to have his local A.A. chapter hold its next meeting here if he missed his train again."

He reached the unwanted customer, swung him around and propelled him to the door. This time he walked him to the street and headed him in the right direction.

Liddell contemplated the advisability of matching the commuter's happy condition, decided no amount of liquor would shake him out of the mood he was in. He took a deep swallow from his glass, went back to studying his reflection in the mirror. It didn't help his mood a bit.

Somewhere, a telephone jangled. The bartender headed for it.

"Probably his old lady," he grumbled. "Wouldn't surprise me to see her come marching in with an ax some night if she can find parking space for her broom." He lifted the receiver to his ear, said hello with a voice that indicated he was prepared for the worst. He grunted, looked down to where Liddell sat.

"For you," he called in a disgusted tone.

Liddell finished his drink, walked the length of the bar, took the receiver.

"How about getting an extension of your own put in?" the man behind the stick grumbled. "You get more calls here than I do."

"You ought to be glad. You thought it was the guy's old lady."

"Yeah, but I had it all figured out what I was going to say to her. This way, I don't get to use it."

Liddell grinned at him, put the receiver to his ear. "Liddell."

The voice on the other end was the husky kind that does things to the spine. "This is Lee Loomis. I don't know if you know me—"

"*The* Lee Loomis?"

There was a pleased sound from the other end of the phone. "A Lee Loomis. I hope it's the one you mean."

"You headlined the show at the Cuernavaca a couple of months ago? That Lee Loomis?"

"How nice of you to remember."

"How could I forget?"

"Then that makes things easier. I want you to do me a favor."

Liddell nodded. "You have it."

"I'd like you to drop by my apartment. Tonight. It'll be worth your while."

"Tonight?" Liddell consulted his watch, saw it to be after eleven. "It's sort of after office hours."

"I'm leaving for the Coast in the morning."

"Oh well, we've got a lousy union anyway. How about in half an hour?"

"I'd be very grateful. I'm at the Haddon Arms. On 47th Street."

Liddell said, "I know the place. I'll be there in a half

hour." He dropped the receiver onto its hook, looked into the envious face of the bartender.

"The Lee Loomis?" the man behind the stick wanted to know.

Liddell nodded.

The bartender shook his head sadly. "That voice alone could do it to me. You going to see her tonight?"

"She couldn't wait."

"Nothing like that ever happens to me. One minute you're standing here looking like you lost your last friend. Next minute a dish like that Loomis dame calls you and insists you come over and see her." He looked Liddell over from head to foot critically, seemed unimpressed. "What've you got that I haven't got?"

"Talent." Liddell winked lewdly.

The bartender bobbed his head grudgingly. "Must be. But it sure doesn't show." He picked up the bill Liddell dropped on the bar, shuffled over to the cash register, rang it up. He returned with some change, spilled it on the bar, watched enviously as Liddell walked to the door.

After Johnny had disappeared into the street, the bartender reached under the bar, came up with a damp rag, started swabbing the bar with circular motions. After a moment, he stopped, stared at the door thoughtfully.

"Even so, I wonder how he advertises it."

Her voice had been sultry and throaty over the phone. When she opened the door in response to Johnny Liddell's knock, it was obvious that the voice belonged.

She was tall. Her red hair was piled on top of her head and a green silk gown did its best to cover her lush figure. Her lips were full, moist, soft; her eyes green and slightly slanted.

10

"So you're Johnny Liddell?" The slanted eyes hopscotched from the broad shoulders to the rugged planes of the face approvingly. "Thanks for coming." She stood aside, took his hand as he walked in.

"I ran all the way," he told her.

She grinned at him, led the way into a living room that had hundreds of counterparts in furnished apartments all over the city. As she walked, her hips worked smoothly against the fragile fabric of the gown. It was highly debatable whether she wore anything under it.

"Like a drink? I could sure use one," she told him.

Liddell nodded, dropped onto the couch, watched her until she disappeared into the kitchen. When she returned, the movement from the front was equally satisfying. She set the bottle and glasses down on a small table in front of the couch, sat down alongside him.

"I really am grateful that you could come on such short notice. This means a lot to me."

"Suppose you fill me in."

The redhead caught her lower lip between her teeth, worried it. "Actually, what I'm going to ask you is a favor for a friend. Not for me." She leaned over, with devastating effect on the low neckline of her gown, spilled some liquor into each of the glasses. "I want you to take on an assignment for him." She straightened up, handed Liddell a glass.

Liddell took his drink, swirled the liquor around the sides of the glass, scowled. "Why doesn't this friend of yours ask me to take the case himself?"

The redhead picked up her glass, sipped at it. "He doesn't think you'd be willing to do him a favor. He thinks you might do it for me."

"And this friend?"

"Mike Klein. In Las Palmas."

11

"Fat Mike?" Liddell grimaced. "He's right. I wouldn't do him a favor." He eyed the girl tentatively. "Why should you?"

The redhead met his gaze levelly. "In my business, Mike Klein is an important man. He runs his own place in Las Palmas, has his finger in half a dozen other spots around the country." She shrugged. "Matter of fact, I'm opening at his Music Hall in Las Palmas the day after tomorrow. It would mean a lot to me if I could bring you back with me."

Liddell took a deep swallow from his glass, set it down. "What's the job?"

The redhead picked two cigarettes from a humidor, lit them, passed one to Liddell. "A friend of his, Larry Adams, was murdered—"

"Adams murdered? When?"

The girl shrugged. "Mike will tell you all about it. He tried to reach you last night, your answering service wouldn't give out any number. This morning your office gave him the same kind of a runaround. So I caught the three o'clock flight in. Funny thing. Your answering service told me where to find you without an argument."

Liddell grinned. "My answering service is a very understanding soul. She probably figured I'd be more simpatico with a voice like yours than with a croak like Fat Mike's." He stared at the girl. "He wants the killer?"

The redhead nodded.

"How about the police department? Isn't that their job?"

The redhead twisted her mouth into a moue of disgust. "The Las Palmas Police Department? All it's good for is to beat up drifters and discourage moochers. They wouldn't know where to begin to look for a killer."

"How come Fat Mike wants me? We've never belonged to the same mutual admiration society."

12

Lee Loomis grinned at him. "You've got Mike all wrong. He thinks you're quite a man." She reached for her purse on a near-by table, pulled out a roll of bills. She flipped through them, letting him see the denominations. "Ten thousand dollars' worth of man."

Liddell whistled noiselessly. "That's a lot of man."

The redhead's eyes measured him frankly. "Mike's a pretty good judge, I'd say." She returned the bills to her bag. "You get five now and five when you deliver the killer."

Liddell fought a losing battle to keep his eyes off the bulging handbag. He tried to compute how many tin coffeepots he'd have to guard at wedding receptions, how many suspicious wives would demand proof of how their Other Half loves and who, for five thousand dollars. The coffeepots and the suspicious wives dropped the decision. "When would he want me to begin this investigation?"

The redhead wrinkled her nose in a grin. "It just so happens there's a direct flight from Idlewild at ten in the morning." She dug into her bag, came up with two American Airlines envelopes. "I'm going back on that flight, and just on the chance you'd be going with me, I bought a ticket for you."

Liddell took a deep drag on his cigarette. "It's only about twelve now. I guess I could clear up everything I have to clear up by then."

The redhead leaned back, jutted her breasts against her robe. Liddell fought a losing struggle to keep his eyes on her face, lost it happily. "Why can't we leave from here? Couldn't you clean up whatever has to be cleaned up by phone from Las Palmas?"

Liddell pursed his lips, considered. He reached over, freshened the half-filled glasses. "That's almost ten hours."

The redhead reached for her glass, with the same happy effect on the neckline as when she had poured the drinks. She lifted her glass to her lips, turned the full effect of the slanted eyes on him from above the rim. "I have no intention of letting you out of my sight until I get you aboard that plane."

Liddell struggled to look unhappy, didn't quite make it.

The redhead dropped expertly tinted eyelids to half veil the slanted green eyes. "I know you weren't counting on being cooped up with me for ten hours. But I'll try not to be too much trouble."

She wasn't.

THREE

In the short space of ten years Las Palmas had grown from a godforsaken, sunbaked spot in the desert to a resort boasting of lush, luxurious hotels that spilled shade and air conditioning into the dry air. Over the years it had become an oasis for outcasts from other parts of the country where open warrants had made a return home inadvisable. Nevada might be willing to overlook certain differences with the law. But New York, Chicago and even Miami had longer memories.

So Las Palmas had become home to a lot of the "boys." They sat around at night and talked of the old times and old places with the sad knowledge that they were now out of bounds. And that knowledge made the nostalgia even greater.

By day they stared morosely at the cottony white clouds that hung motionless in the blue skies and wondered what it would be like to feel a cutting November wind again. Sometimes they even thought longingly of walking down State Street when the gutters were ankle deep in slush and the wind roared off the lake like a stagestruck banshee.

Fat Mike Klein was one of the boys who couldn't go home. Many times over the past few years he wished he had seen the last of the modern pastel-colored buildings, the neon lights and the blistering sun that spelled Las Palmas. But his face was too well known to the homicide squads of at least four cities; and the dry air, the monotony of the perfect weather, the desert wind that dried the perspiration on his body—these were preferable to the even greater monotony of Sing Sing, Joliet or Alcatraz. As long as there had to be a prison, Fat Mike grudgingly preferred the gaudier one—Las Palmas—although sometimes it felt almost as confining.

Fat Mike sat in his office behind the casino in the New York Music Hall, stared dyspeptically at the orange-red rim as dawn broke over the black bulk of the mountains across the desert. He was fat, soft looking. As he sat watching the sky brighten into a spectrum of colors, he made and broke tiny bubbles in the center of his pouty lips. His hands were laced across his midsection, dimples where the knuckles should have been. Only the black disks of his eyes, buttressed by discolored pouches and heavily-veined lids gave any hint of the meatball who. had once run the East River docks for Arty MacFarland and had kept the river well stocked with the corpses of insurgents who had "lost their footing." It wasn't until the D.A.'s office had shown undue curiosity in the number of longshoremen who went swimming at odd hours that Fat Mike had decamped for warmer climates.

There was a knock at the door. Fat Mike grunted, swung around. His voice had a choked effect, as though his three chins made talking an effort. "Come in."

A uniformed deputy sheriff stuck his head in the door. "Regan's here, chief."

Fat Mike nodded, spilled the chins over his collar. "Send him in."

The Deputy yanked his head out of the doorway,

pushed the door open. Sheriff Regan walked in, closed the door behind him. He was still on the right side of sixty, his thick white hair contrasted sharply with the black eyebrows and black mustache.

"I got your message, Mike. It's been pretty busy, so—"

Fat Mike cut him off with a gesture, motioned to a chair. "You found nothing." It was a statement, not a question.

Regan raked at his hair with clenched fingers. "Hell, we've only started looking. There were a lot of people who wanted Larry out of the way. It'll take time."

The heavily-veined lids drooped over the fat man's eyes. He looked almost asleep. "We don't have time. I'm bringing in a special investigator to handle this."

The sheriff walked over to the desk, leaned his knuckles on it. "I don't get it. This isn't the first guy who got hit—"

Fat Mike didn't open his eyes. "It's the first one who got hit we didn't know about it in advance." The eyes slowly opened. "We don't like for somebody to be handing out contracts without he gets our okay. Especially when it's one of us."

"What makes you think it's a contract hit? It could be—"

The fat man shook his head, disturbing the rolls of fat. "Only a pro could have done that job. You think the average Joe, he loses his roll at the table, he tries to get even with the guy who runs the Casino?" He shook his head again. "Somebody bought that hit and wanted to advertise it."

Perspiration gleamed on the sheriff's face in spite of the fact that the air conditioning was on full. He pulled a balled handkerchief from his hip pocket, swabbed at his face.

There were advantages to Las Palmas other than the fact that it offered a home away from home for lammisters. That advantage was Sheriff Tom Regan. Under him, law enforcement was satisfyingly broadminded. While mobsters, murderers, prostitutes and panderers were free to appear openly at its clubs and casinos, transients with no visible means of support found that the arm of the law could clamp down with authority and speed. The only unforgivable crime in Las Palmas was to be broke—and its citizens and operators approved.

Sheriff Tom Regan had started his career as a member of New York's Finest. His father, a political district captain in the 23rd Assembly District in Brownsville, had seen to it that his son didn't waste too much time pounding a beat and less than a year after he made the Force, he was assigned to Inspector Charley Wilson of the vice squad operating in Brighton Beach. Regan was a fast study, and by the time the Amen investigation sent Inspector Charley Wilson to his attic one night to make an unsuccessful attempt to swallow his service revolver, young Tom Regan emptied out his safe-deposit boxes and shook the dust of New York from his feet once and for all.

The mob never forgets its benefactors. When Tom Regan showed up in Florida a few years later, he was assigned as chief of security in one of the mob's hotels along the beach. As a hotel dick, Regan managed to make new friends, new connections. His take from the hookers who worked the hotel, his cut from the sneak thieves who rolled Johns who were in no position to yell copper, his take from the floating crap game that made its headquarters in his hotel made his stay in Florida profitable if not inspiring.

The trek west started after the war with the opening

of Las Vegas and Reno to legal gambling. Tom Regan again emptied his safe-deposit boxes and followed the trend. In Las Vegas, his reputation had preceded him and he found a lukewarm welcome, in Reno no welcome at all. The word was out that operations were to go on the legit and a twister like Regan could never be depended on to keep his fingers from getting sticky.

As Vegas and Reno made their clean-up stick, there were others like Tom Regan—croupiers who tried to run a crooked game, 21 dealers who played from the top and bottom with equal impartiality, stickmen who tried to run in flats, hustlers who gave the town a bad name and chased away the family trade—all these continued to move on. In Las Palmas they found a playground conveniently located for both the sports from below the border as well as the Hollywood crowd who were on the prowl for less regulated and less publicized revelry.

There had been deaths in Las Palmas, mostly suicides. But even these had been held to a minimum. The casinos hired experienced men, officers who kept an eye peeled for a likely case; periodic patrolling of the grounds and out of the way places had prevented a number of unpleasant incidents. In a couple of cases crooked employees had had to be taught a lesson for the benefit of the others, but these hits had been okayed by the operators and never took place within the town limits of Las Palmas.

Tom Regan knew the fat man was right when he said the Larry Evans kill was different. He swabbed at his glistening face again.

"Give us a chance to crack it first, before you bring in any outsiders, Mike," he urged. "This is my town and I don't want any—"

"This is our town," the fat man told him coldly.

"Mine, Morrow's, Lewine's, Sommers's and Rossi's. You just work here. You know?" The voice was low, but there was a thin edge of menace in it.

The sheriff tried to outstare the fat man, lost the contest, dropped his eyes first. "I just meant I had the town under good control. Some outsider coming in might upset things."

"It's up to you to see he don't. He's coming for only one thing. To find whoever it was killed Larry, Adams."

"When does he get here?"

The fat man grunted at the necessity for movement, checked his wristwatch. "He leaves at ten New York time. He should be here some time this afternoon."

"Do I know this guy?"

Fat Mike shrugged, spilling his jowls over his collar. "It don't matter. I do. His name is Johnny Liddell. I know him from the old days."

"You're the boss, Mike. Whatever you say goes. But what makes you think the killer is still in town?"

The man behind the desk reached into the humidor for a cigar, tested it between his thumb and forefinger for freshness. "Because he's a local." He bit the end off the cigar, spat it at the wastebasket. "He's got to be."

"Why?"

Fat Mike stuck the cigar between his teeth, chewed on it for a moment before answering. "You're not much of a cop, Regan—" He lifted his hand to stave off an objection. "We like it that way. What I started out to say, there's one thing you do real good. No one comes into this town on a plane or a train you don't know about. No one registers in a hotel or a motel you don't have a run-down. So if a pro came into this town and spent three, four days casing Larry's place you'd know."

Globules of perspiration glistened on the forehead and the upper lip of the white-haired man. "Suppose he just drove in, filled the contract and drove out again?"

The fat man chewed on his cigar contemplatively, shook his head. "That means he had the whole layout of Larry Adams's house pat in his mind. He walks right into the study, makes the hit, walks right out. He knows where to park his car, he knows right where the French doors are, he knows right where to cross the lawn and not be seen." He shook his head again, wagging his jowls. "He knows too goddam much for a guy who just drives in and drives right out again. You know?"

Regan pulled a balled handkerchief from his pocket, swabbed at his streaming jowls. "I haven't had a report on anyone who looks like a button."

"Keep checking. Maybe he's in town weeks, even." Fat Mike leaned back, appeared to go to sleep. "How about the medical report?"

"Heart attack. The coroner issued the certificate."

"The other details?"

Regan nodded. "We're taking care of everything in the morning. We cleared with Adams's half sister. She's the only relative he's got. All she wanted to know was how much money he left and how much of it she gets."

"Figures. And his broad?"

"We gave her some dough, told her to get out of town and keep going. By now she's probably a blonde, changed her name and has put a thousand miles between her and here."

The fat man chuckled deep in his chest. He opened his eyes, sat up. "So far so good." He swung his chair around, slid open a panel that revealed a built-in refrigerator and a miniature bar. "Too early for a drink?"

"One would go real good right now," Regan admitted. "It's been a long night." He watched while the fat man dumped some ice into two glasses, then put them on his desk and reached for a bottle.

"Say when."

The sheriff let him pour a full two fingers of scotch over the ice before he stopped him. He reached for his glass. The coolness felt good against his palm. He waited until the fat man had poured his own drink.

"How can you be sure this Liddell won't stir things up by doing a lot of talking?"

The fat man balanced his cigar on the edge of the ash tray. "What could he prove?" He wiped the wet smear of his mouth with the back of his hand anticipatory to taking a drink. "I just want him to verify a few suspicions I got. That's what I'm paying for."

FOUR

At the airport in Las Palmas, Johnny Liddell and the redhead picked up the car she had parked there the day before on her way to New York. He drove it around to the baggage stand, collected their bags.

"You want to drive, Johnny?" the redhead asked. "A lot of men seem to think a woman's place is not behind the wheel."

Liddell grinned at her. "There are more appropriate places."

The redhead gave him instructions to Mike Klein's Music Hall, leaned back against the cushions as he expertly wheeled the big convertible toward the highway.

"I don't think we'll be seeing much of each other while we're in Las Palmas, Johnny," she told him. "I don't think it would be a good idea."

"Why not? Fat Mike?"

The redhead didn't answer for a second, finally said, "That's right."

"Why?"

"You know how it is. Mike wants the other boys to think I'm private property. If you and I—"

Liddell grunted. "So what? So why should a dish like

you have to play house with a fat slob like him? He sent you to New York to get me down here, didn't he?"

The redhead stared up at the sky, nodded. "I played that ad lib, Johnny. He figured the ten thousand would be the bait. The rest of the script I made up as we went along." She turned her face toward him. "Mike is important to me, Johnny. I want you to understand."

"Forget it."

She reached out, laid her hand on his arm. "No. I want you to understand. I don't mean anything to him except I'm good for his ego. He likes word to get around that I'm his girl." She rolled her head back, stared up at the skies. "Outside of that, he doesn't know whether I'm a man or woman."

For the next few miles they were silent. The road wound through a colony of medium-sized estates, discreetly screened by high hedges and curving driveways. Here and there, Liddell caught a glimpse of Spanish style houses with heavy tiled roofs. Las Palmas's exiles apparently made their cells as bearable as possible.

Finally, the redhead broke the silence. "I'm not trying to cop a plea, Johnny. But I wish you could understand. You would if you knew the story of my life. It's not a very pretty one. But sitting here, thinking about it, I know I'd do it the same way if I had it to do over again."

"Even knowing what you do about Fat Mike and how he gets his money?"

The redhead shrugged. "So he's a gambler. I hear stories about how he kept the boys in line on the docks and didn't care how he had to do it. What's that to me? He always treated me good. I don't care how he got his money. The important thing is that he's got it. It's not a very easy commodity to lay your hands on. I

24

should know—I broke enough fingernails scratching for it in my time."

She closed her eyes, remembered the days of waiting on tables, hoofing in second-class night clubs and filling in as a bar hostess in clip joints.

"I finally made the chorus line at the Stardust in Vegas three or four years ago. Back line. All of us were on the lookout for those characters who are supposed to light their cigars with hundred-dollar bills. Joey Knight is headlining this particular night. He happens to mention that Mike Klein, the big labor guy, is out front." She chuckled. "I'd heard all about these labor guys. They light their cigars with thousand-dollar bills. So I made up my mind to get next to him."

"That would be a good trick in itself," Liddell said.

"I was a redhead and Mike is a sucker for redheads." She laced her fingers at the back of her neck. "First thing I know, I'm out of the chorus and Mike is picking up the tab for me to take singing lessons. He tells me he's out of the labor racket and is going to take over a place in Las Palmas. He wants me to break in my act in a couple of little spots. Then he got me a crack at a place in Chicago where he has an interest. Once I got going good, he set it up for me to work the whole circuit—the Cuernavaca in New York, the Chez in Chicago, Amo's in Hollywood—and now the Music Hall. You don't think I owe it to a guy who's done that for me to let him wear me on his arm and show me around as his?"

"How long you got to serve down here?"

The redhead grinned. "Three weeks with no time off for good behavior. But I'll be coming back to New York next month." She rolled her head over, studied his profile. "Interested?"

25

"Look me up."

The character of the neighborhood was changing from the lush residential district to an area of restaurants and honky-tonks. Behind them, in the distance, the harsh rock outlines of the mountains were softened by an afternoon heat haze. A little farther along, Restaurant Row gave way to the Strip, a mile of casinos and luxury hotels, their porte-cocheres and parking lots already filled.

Lee Loomis pointed to a sprawling, low, white stone building at the far end of the Strip. "That's the Music Hall, the salt mine where I'll be working," she told him. "I hope you're coming to the opening tonight?"

Liddell favored the building with a jaundiced eye. "Look but don't touch, huh?"

"You make it seem so permanent." Lee grinned. "Three weeks isn't forever."

Liddell swung the car onto the porte-cochere of the Music Hall, braked to a stop at the entrance. A uniformed bellboy materialized at the side door, grinned at the redhead.

"Hi, Miss Loomis. Welcome back."

"Thanks, Eddie." She let him open the door for her, got out. "My bags are in the back. You know where they go. I think Mr. Liddell will be staying here. Check the desk where to put his stuff, will you, like a good kid?"

The bellboy bobbed his head, loped in the direction of the registration desk.

Liddell stood alongside the car for a moment, let the dry desert breeze cool him. Then he followed the redhead into the casino.

The air conditioning hit him in the face like a wet rag as he stepped inside. The 21 tables and slots were getting a moderate play, but the craps layouts were practically deserted—the heavy play at the felt-covered tables

26

usually started when the big players finished their 8 p.m. breakfast to fortify them for a long night.

The redhead led the way through an aisle of slot machines, where men and women of all sizes and shapes were feeding coins of all denominations into the machines' maw with feverish concentration. Not once as they traversed the long lane did one of the machines pay off.

At the rear of the casino, a uniformed deputy replete with whipcords, .45 on his hip, badge on his tunic, lounged against the wall next to a door marked *Private*. He straightened up as the redhead walked up, favored her with a warm smile. Some of the warmth drained out of it as he looked past her to Liddell.

"Mike is expecting Mr. Liddell, Tommy," she told him.

The deputy opened the door, stuck his head in, murmured something. The door opened, a man in his shirtsleeves walked out. Black halfmoons of sweat ringed his armpits, little beads of perspiration glistened on his upper lip. He rolled the macerated end of a toothpick from one corner of his mouth to the other as he looked the redhead over from head to foot with appropriate stops on the way.

"Well, well. Welcome home, honey."

"Where's Mike?" The coldness in the girl's voice was unmistakable.

The man in the doorway looked past her to Liddell. "And you must be the shamus." He pulled the toothpick from between his teeth, eyed the crushed end incuriously. "Funny thing the boss has to send for somebody all the way from New York when he has some real talent around here, huh, Tommy?" he addressed the uniformed deputy. His eyes rolled up to Liddell. "Thompson here was a New York flattie before his health kicked up. You'd figure that was enough talent, wouldn't you?"

"Don't tell me your troubles, friend," Liddell snapped. "You didn't send for me. Fat Mike did—"

The man with the toothpick looked pained. "Mr. Klein," he corrected. "Isn't that right, Tommy? We treat the boss with respect." He looked back at Liddell. "Mr. Klein isn't here."

"Now, wait a minute, Whitey. When I left for New York yesterday Mike told me to bring Liddell here—" Lee started to argue.

Whitey shrugged elaborately. "Nobody tells me nothing. All I know is arrangements have been changed. They're all meeting at Sommers's penthouse." He stuck the toothpick back between his teeth, chewed on it. "Something might have come up." He shrugged again. "Nobody tells me nothing."

"Have somebody drive him over then. You know Mike hates to be kept waiting," the redhead said.

Whitey appeared to consider it, agreed. "Why didn't I think of that? Have somebody drive him over, Tommy," he snapped at the deputy. He looked Liddell over from head to foot. "I hear you got quite a reputation, shamus. You might need more than a reputation in this town." He bobbed his head. "A lot more." He let his eyes flick hungrily over the redhead. "Isn't that right, baby?"

"One of these days you're going to look at me like that and you're going to wish you hadn't," Lee Loomis told him.

The man in the doorway pasted a smile on his thin lips. "Never worry about anyone looking, chick. Start worrying when they stop." He turned and shut the door behind him.

28

"The local representative of the Welcome Wagon?" Liddell wanted to know.

"Don't pay any attention to him," the redhead replied. "He's just burned because Mike called for outside help." She turned to the deputy. "Will you see that Liddell gets over to the penthouse, Tommy?"

"Sure, Miss Loomis. This way, Mac." He turned, Liddell followed as the deputy cut a way through the clotted slot-machine players with his broad shoulders.

FIVE

The Las Palmas Arms was an expensive pile of mortar and plate glass that towered over all the other buildings on the Strip. The lobby was furnished in aggressively modern style. Brightly-colored couches and chrome chairs tastefully complemented the soft, ankle-deep carpeting. The western motif was evidenced by the bas-relief figures of bucking broncos and ranch scenes that decorated the walls.

The deputy who had been delegated to drive Liddell from the Music Hall led the way across the lobby to a registration desk where a man in a western style shirt was blowing his nose noisily in an oversized handkerchief. He stowed the handkerchief in his hip pocket, watched the deputy and Liddell approach through rheumy eyes.

"Will you call the penthouse, tell them the man they're expecting is down here?"

The clerk looked Liddell over again, nodded. He walked to a small switchboard, plugged in a wire, held the receiver to his ear. He muttered a few words into the mouthpiece, broke the connection. He nodded to the deputy. "He's to go right up."

30

Johnny Liddell thanked the deputy for the lift, turned and crossed the lobby to the bank of elevators. A small brass plaque alongside the end one read: *Penthouse Only.*

Liddell stepped into the cage, pushed the button. A man in a wrinkled seersucker suit got up leisurely from a chair facing the elevators, walked into the cage.

"Looks like it's out of order," Liddell grunted. "I pushed the button, nothing happened."

The man reached past him, snapped a switch. "Works better with the current on." The doors whooshed softly shut, the elevator started smoothly upward.

Liddell turned to face the man, who was leaning against the back wall of the cage. His eyes were tired, his suit wrinkled, but the right hand sunk in the pocket of his jacket gave him authority.

"What is this?" Liddell wanted to know.

"Got a call from Whitey at the Music Hall. He spotted the betsy." He reached over, flipped back Liddell's jacket, exposing the .45 in its holster. "You won't be needing that on a social call."

"Who're you?"

"The welcoming committee," the tired-eyed man drawled. He nodded to the gun. "Take it out with your left hand. Two fingers."

Liddell shrugged, lifted the .45 out with the thumb and forefinger of his left hand, passed it to the other man. The man in the seersucker suit weighed it on the flat of his palm, grunted, "Heavy piece."

"Makes my coat hang straight."

"You'll get it back on the way out," the other man told him placidly.

The elevator glided to a smooth stop at the penthouse floor, the doors slid open. Liddell scowled at his co-passenger, stepped out. The tired-eyed man was leaning comfortably against the rear wall as the doors cut him off from view.

Liddell made a few pointed comments at the closed doors, then walked over to the door with the letter *A* stenciled on it in gilt.

A thin, lanky man whose sandy hair had receded from his brow, exposing a freckled pate, stood in the doorway. He looked Liddell over incuriously, stepped aside to permit him to enter.

Liddell walked into a large, tastefully-appointed living room with picture windows on both sides. One gave an uninterrupted view of the desert with the blue-black mountain range beyond; the other looked out over the multicolored lights, the flashing neons and the sprawling pastel buildings of the Strip, their pools glistening in the sunlight like oddly-shaped bits of mirror.

The thin man closed the door behind them. "You're late."

"Yeah. That customs inspection you got in this place takes time."

A dark-haired, pleasant-looking man got up from a long, low couch where he had been leafing through the pages of *Esquire,* and came over, hand extended. "You must be Liddell. I'm Martin Sommers. I hope our security man didn't annoy you. It's just a precaution."

Liddell took his hand, released it, looked around.

Two other men who had apparently been engaged in a private conversation, drew apart, stared at Liddell incuriously.

"You know my associates?" He indicated the thin, lantern-jawed man who had opened the door. "Eddie Morrow. He operates the Cash Box on the Strip." He turned to the two men standing apart. "Al Rossi and Benny Lewine. Mike Klein is on his way."

"Why the reception committee?" Liddell wanted to know.

Sommers shrugged. "We're all in this together." He indicated the portable bar near the picture window. "Care for a drink while you're waiting?"

"Scotch on the rocks," Liddell said. While Lewine walked over to the bar and started making the drink, Liddell turned back to Sommers. "The counselor? That Marty Sommers?"

The tall man smiled a smile that failed to reach his eyes. "You have a good memory, Liddell. I hope you forget as well as you remember?" His skin was a mahogany color, wrinkles dug white trenches in the tan when he smiled. "That was a long time ago."

Martin Sommers had been the leading gang mouthpiece in Chicago a few years before, batting a thousand in keeping his clients out of jail. When Albie Morris violated the mob's rule to stay clean with Mr. Whiskers and got tagged with an income-tax rap, he called for Sommers.

On the face of it, it was a simple one. Just a case of having jurisdiction switched to southern Illinois where a copy of the Federal jury panel was available. The list of prospective jurors was split up among four men who sifted it carefully to make sure of a friendly and co-operative panel. The only taboo was—no money must pass hands. But Albie Morris tried to copper his bet by buying two of the jurors without taking his counsel into his confidence.

The bought jurors tried so hard to earn their fee that an enraged Federal district attorney screamed for an investigation. The two jurors sang loud and long.

Martin Sommers escaped with disbarment when the D.A. failed to prove his knowledge of the bribe. Albie Morris had broken the mob's rules twice, so his sentence was more to the point. He was found parked in his car on a deserted lane, his lungs full of carbon monoxide. The coroner's jury called it suicide. No one bothered to explain how he had committed suicide with no hose in the car. No one really asked. But Martin Sommers, no longer useful to the mob, decided that a change of scenery was in the cards. They gave him management of the Desert Sands.

Liddell accepted his drink from Benny Lewine. "It's a long way from Seventh Avenue, Benny."

Lewine shrugged. "I never noticed." He still bore the marks of his original profession. At one time a leading lightweight, Benny had rebelled against the orders from above to go into the tank. A squad of goons with lead pipes convinced him. They also convinced him he was in the wrong racket. He became one of Sam Morris's enforcers in the garment district. When an honest labor union leader was found beaten to death in a telephone booth, it seemed advisable for Benny Lewine, who had been seen near the booth, to seek greener pastures.

Liddell smelled the drink, took a taste. It tasted as good as it smelled. "The redhead forgot to mention this was a community effort. Was there anything else she forgot to tell me?"

"Such as?"

Liddell shrugged. "Such as why you really sent for me. She told me Larry Adams was murdered. There wasn't a line in any of the papers."

Martin Sommers brought a cigarette holder from his breast pocket, blew through it. "Larry was murdered all right. We managed to keep it out of the papers." He brought a cigarette from his jacket pocket, screwed it into the holder. "A story like that would be bad for a town like this. People might get the idea that it's the

34

old days all over again, violence and all. It would be bad for business."

Liddell nodded. "Any objection to my seeing the body?"

The tanned man smiled easily, the sides of his eyes crinkling whitely. "It hadn't occurred to us you'd want to." He tilted the holder from the corner of his mouth. "You see, Larry was an Orthodox Jew, which necessitated burying him today. He had always expressed the desire to be cremated, so—" He shrugged expressively.

"So you cremated him. And now you're willing to pay me ten thousand to find his killer. Even though there's nothing you can prosecute him on. Why?"

"Why what?"

"Why should this killer be worth ten thousand? I wouldn't figure any of you to be shocked ten grand worth by a hit."

Sommers smiled bleakly. "Would it seem more reasonable to you if I explained one of us might be next?" He turned to Al Rossi. "Call Mike's place, find out what's keeping him." He turned back to Liddell. "Since Mike was the one who brought you into this, I'd like him to be here when I explain."

Rossi picked up the phone from the desk, dialed a number. He was a short, heavy-set man dressed in a black silk suit that had been tailored in Hong Kong, a white on white shirt and a white silk tie. His thick hair was shot with gray, he had a nervous habit of clenching his teeth in a way that made the muscles along his jaw stand out like bunches of grapes. He finally shook his head, hung up. "No answer."

Eddie Morrow, the thin, lantern-jawed man who had let Liddell in, walked over to the bar, helped himself to a drink. "So he's on his way over. Let's get started. Fat Mike don't need no fill-in. Liddell does."

Sommers chewed on the cigarette holder, looked around. The other men nodded or shrugged. "We might as well." He motioned to Liddell. "Pull up a chair." He waited while Johnny dropped into it. "Naturally, what we say here doesn't go out of this room."

Liddell nodded.

"We have reason to believe that Adams was killed as an example to the rest of us. Any one of us in this room, or all of us, could be next."

"You must have an active Civic Improvement League in this town," Liddell suggested.

"Look, shamus," Lewine growled, "to you it may be funny. To us, it's serious. Ten grand worth. Remember?"

"You expect me to believe someone is going to check you out, one by one?" Liddell asked. He held up his glass. "You ought to dilute this stuff if that's the way it affects you."

Sommers waved the ex-pug to silence. "I know how ridiculous it sounds, but the fact is that we've all been put on notice that unless we get up a kitty of a million dollars, we stand to be killed one by one."

Liddell stared at him, realized the man was serious. "You mean someone is trying to sell you protection? A million dollars' worth? Why, in the old days—"

"That was the old days. This ain't the old days," Benny Lewine chimed in. "Back then, nobody even walked on the same side of the street with us without he tips his hat. Today it's different. Today a lot of fresh young punks think they can take over. They figure us for has-beens, soft touches. Young punks!"

Liddell pursed his lips, cocked his head. "Al Capone was a young punk once to Big Jim. Charley Lucky was a young punk once to Joe the Boss. They grow up fast, sometimes, these young punks," he conceded. "Still it's crazy."

"Sure it's crazy," Eddie Morrow snapped. "But there's a lot of crazy people. How do you handle crazy people, how do you figure them?"

Liddell stared from man to man in the room thoughtfully, saw they actually had been shaken by Adams's murder. These were men who, in the old days, had dealt with Death as a commodity to be bought or sold for a price. Now, after years of soft living, they were on the wrong side of the counter and they were scared.

He realized another thing—these weren't the same men he had known years before. Even Benny Lewine, whose awesome scowl had stricken more than one witness with a case of amnesia, was changed. His face was still battered, his ears still twisted bits of cartilage attached to the side of his skull. But the scrambled features were softened by an overlay of fat. The eyes were still flat, lusterless marbles peering from under thickened brows and masses of scar tissue. But the soft pouches under them took away from the old menace.

"How'd you get the demand for this million-dollar kitty?"

Martin Sommers dug into his breast pocket, brought out a folded sheet of paper, handed it over to Liddell. "We all got this identical letter. Adams too."

Liddell set down his drink, unfolded the sheet of paper. It was typed single space. The message was brief and to the point:

> *You been doing real good, so I'm cutting myself in. My share is a cool million but I'm going to be real easy. Six of you split it even—Adams, Klein, Rossi, Lewine, Morrow and Sommers.*

Anything happens to one of you, the share goes up. You'll be hearing from the other boys, then you'll be hearing from me.

Liddell rubbed the paper between thumb and fore-finger. It was a cheap grade of typewriter paper that would probably be on sale in every five and dime in the country, impossible to trace.

"When did you get this?"

"About a week ago."

Liddell picked up his drink, took a deep swallow. "But you did nothing about it until now?"

Sommers looked around the room before answering. "Would you? You said yourself it sounded crazy. We just told our boys to keep their eyes open for anything funny or anybody acting crazy. Crank stuff, you know?"

"Then Larry Adams gets hit and you start figuring it's something to worry about." He looked from face to face. "The sheriff in on this?"

Al Rossi spoke up for the first time. "If we wanted the sheriff in on it we wouldn't need you. Me"—he hit his chest with the flat of his hand—"I don't even buy having you in on it. Word gets out we have to send for outside help to handle a shake, every petty larceny hustler in the country will be out trying his luck."

Rossi had worked with Buggsy Siegel long before the Bug had transferred his activities to the West Coast. He went all the way back to when Siegel had masterminded the troop in Brownsville that was to make history as Murder, Inc.

The night the Bug sat on the couch in Virginia Hill's Beverly Hills home and fielded a full charge of buckshot with the back of his skull, Al Rossi was hosting a party at the Hollywood Roosevelt Hotel ten miles away. Since it was generally understood that Rossi was the Bug's bodyguard, there were a lot of unanswered questions. After that Rossi found his welcome home to Las Vegas, where Siegel was a big operator, something less than cordial. So he had joined the trek to Las Palmas.

"I say it's crackpot stuff and the hell with it," Rossi concluded.

Eddie Morrow whirled on him. "So how did Larry sprout all them holes in his chest? Termites?"

"There were a lot of guys who'd like to spit on his grave. So maybe this just plays into the creep's hands. He figures we think he's behind the hit so he turns on the pressure. Crackpot stuff!" Rossi argued.

"Pressure?" Liddell looked from Rossi to Sommers. "You've heard from him again?"

Sommers nodded. "I got a call this morning. That's what this meeting is about."

"Young or old, man or woman?" Liddell wanted to know.

The dark-faced man rattled the holder stem against his teeth, shook his head. "I couldn't tell. He held a handkerchief or something over the mouthpiece."

"He?"

Sommers shrugged. "I just don't associate a woman with shakedowns of this kind." He removed the holder, tugged the butt from it, tossed it into an ash tray. "He told me I was elected to make the collection. He'll call back telling us when and where to make the payoff."

Liddell considered it. "Why should he figure the other boys would part with $200,000 to keep you breathing?"

The smile was back, a bit strained. "He doesn't. He wants a million and if he doesn't get it, he's going to cut us down one by one. Only, he's not giving out any hints who'll be next."

"Me, it's worth the dough to keep living," Morrow grumbled. "You guys figure it for a hustle, so I'll go

39

along with bringing in an outside man. But I'm not figuring on swallowing lead because some other guy can't get it up."

Sommers stared at him coldly. "It's not a case of any of us not being able to get up our share, Morrow. It's just—"

The telephone on the table near Sommers shrilled. He picked it up, held it to his ear. His mouth went slack, the cigarette holder dropped from his hand. "Wait a minute—hello, hello." He pounded on the crossbar. "Hello! Hello!"

Finally he dropped the receiver on its hook, looked around.

"The shake artist! He said our share's gone up to $250,000. Now there's only four of us contributing!"

Eddie Morrow looked stricken. There was a noticeable twitch under his right eye. "Fat Mike's dead?"

"That's what he said." Sommers's eyes hopscotched around the room, stopped on Liddell. "What do we do now?"

"We pay, that's what we do," Lewine growled. "Don't ask him. It's not his skin that's going to get punctured. It's ours."

Liddell shrugged. "The man's right. You either pay off or find the guy before anybody else gets hurt." He pulled a cigarette from his pocket, touched a match to it. "Looks like the guy really does mean business. He's following the extortionist pattern. First the letter, time to think it over. Then something to show he means business, then the date for the payoff. Even then, sometimes, he doesn't keep it—just to make sure the cops haven't been run in."

"He knows we're in no position to yell copper," Morrow whined.

Benny Lewine patted the sides of his jowls with

40

a folded pocket handkerchief. "Maybe he's sore we brought in the shamus. You notice it was Fat Mike got hit, and Liddell was his idea. I'm in for my share. I don't want no trouble."

Eddie Morrow raised his glass to his lips with a shaking hand. The twitch under his eyes was more noticeable. "I'm in, too. How do we make the payoff?"

Sommers shook his head. "I don't know. He didn't say."

Liddell said. "He's in no hurry. The longer you have to think about Fat Mike and Larry Adams, the closer you'll follow his instructions. This boy is no amateur."

SIX

Although it was still afternoon and the sun was glaring down with blinding intensity out on the Strip, it was cool and dim in the casino of Mike Klein's Music Hall. Johnny Liddell walked in, headed for the registration desk in the lobby.

"Can you tell me what room Lee Loomis is in?" he asked.

The clerk looked unhappy, wagged his head. "I can't give out any personal information about our entertainers." He looked down at the folded bill Liddell held between his fingers, managed to look even unhappier at the denomination. "It would cost me my job." He looked around, let his eyes return hungrily to the bill, dropped his voice. "If you'd like to meet a girl, I happen to know one who—"

"How about Mike Klein? Where can I find him?"

The clerk seemed to be having difficulty tearing his eyes away from the bill. "He has his office—"

"He's not in his office."

The man behind the desk tore his eyes regretfully from the bill, sighed. "I'm afraid you'll have to wait until he gets back. Mr. Klein never discusses business in his bungalow." He flashed a fond farewell glance at the bill. "This girl, I mentioned—"

"Some other time," Liddell told him. He wandered into the casino, checked the small groups huddled around the 21 tables, the slots, satisfied himself that the redhead wasn't in the casino.

He crossed to the breakfast room, checked on the tables on the flagstone terrace with no success. The chairs that lined the pool, shaded by multicolored umbrellas, were almost deserted; a few deeply-tanned showgirls were broiling their skins in deck chairs, resorting to frequent oilings of sun lotion. The redhead wasn't among them.

As he stood there, one of the girls got up from her deck chair, carefully collected her suntan lotion, her towels and an oversized handbag.

She was stacked.

Liddell stood enjoying the effect as she walked toward him. Her gold-blond hair had a metallic sheen in the sunlight. Her body had a well-oiled glisten that testified to many hours in the sun. Her mouth was a crimson slash.

As she walked, full breasts swayed rhythmically, threatened to negate the restraint of the thin wisp of brassière that was doing a half-hearted job of containing the cantilever construction of her façade. A matching V of bikini was perched perilously low on her hips.

Aware of an audience, she gave her hips just enough extra bounce to prove her assets were as sound as the First National—and just as liquid.

As she came abreast of Liddell and started past him, he stepped toward her. "I beg your pardon."

The snow-top stopped, looked him over coolly. "What for?"

43

"I thought you might be able to help me."

She looked him over again, pursed her lips. "It could be. Depends on what your problem is."

Liddell grinned, debated the urgency of his present mission. The frank look of approval in the blonde's eyes was a strong temptation. He finally dropped the decision. "I'm looking for Mike Klein."

The interest drained from the girl's face. "His office is in the rear of the casino."

"I tried there. They told me he had a bungalow back here. I've forgotten which one."

"Bungalow B. The big one at the far end. Any other problems?"

"If I think of any, I'll be back."

The blonde smiled sweetly, turned and continued in the direction of the smaller bungalows off the pool area. The effect from the flip side was as interesting as it had been from the front.

When the blonde had passed out of sight around the corner of a bungalow, Liddell headed around the pool, climbed the grassy incline that led from the pool area. The bungalow she indicated was larger than the others, set in position to command a view of both the desert and the mountains in the rear, the pool area and the casino from the front. As he walked up to it, Liddell noticed that like all the others, the heavy soundproof curtains were tightly closed. Las Palmas was promoted as a resort of sunshine and scenery, yet all the buildings seemed in conspiracy to block out both.

Liddell rapped at the door, waited for a moment, then knocked again. This time the door was opened by the redhead.

Lee Loomis's jaw sagged when she recognized Liddell. She tried to close the door, but he kept his foot in it. "Johnny, you crazy or something?"

44

"Why don't you let me in? It's better than discussing it out here for the benefit of the neighbors."

The redhead pulled the door open, let him in, closed the door behind him. "Johnny, if Mike catches you here—"

Liddell shook his head. "Mike's going to be tied up solid for quite a while." He stepped into the expensively furnished living room, whistled his appreciation. "Quite a place."

"If you came here to write it up for *House Beautiful*, come back some other time when I'm not here, will you, Johnny?"

"I told you to stop worrying. Didn't Mike tell you he was going to be tied up most of the day?"

"I didn't see him. He was already gone when I got here." The redhead tossed the long red hair out of her face. "It's not that I'm not glad to see you, Johnny. It's just that Mike gets so unreasonable—"

Liddell looked around, walked over to a desk against the far wall. He started flipping through the papers on it. "You don't mind if I make myself at home?" he asked.

The redhead ran over to him, the sway of her breasts under the thin nile-green robe tracing designs on the thin fabric. She caught his arm. "If he caught you near his desk—" She pulled him away. "I already told you he doesn't like people messing with things that belong to him."

"I remember. I'll be real careful."

The redhead shook her head. "He might just walk in and—"

"I doubt it, baby. Fat Mike has walked in here for the last time." His eyes moved around the room, looking for signs of a struggle, found none.

"What's that mean? You think he walked out on me?

45

Think again. His clothes, everything's here. He didn't take a thing with him. He'll be back."

"If they put wheels on him," Liddell grunted. "He was due at the meeting at Sommers's place. He never showed."

The redhead stared at him. "Mike was never very good at keeping appointments. Maybe—"

Liddell shook his head. "There was a phone call saying he was dead. They neglected to say where. But a carcass like Mike's can't stay hidden for long."

"Dead? Murdered?"

Liddell nodded.

"But who?" Lee demanded dumbly. "Mike was an important man. The organization wouldn't let him get killed."

"The same guy who killed Adams, probably. The killer neglected to get permission. A real breach of etiquette. Somebody'll have to talk to him about that." He indicated the closed door leading to the bedroom. "That where he kept his things?"

The redhead nodded dumbly, made no attempt to stop him when Liddell walked to the door, opened it. He satisfied himself that the closets were filled with clothes, the drawers with linens. He walked back into the living room where the girl sat on the couch, drywashing her hands in her lap.

"Mike have a gun?"

The redhead shook her head. "He was scared stiff of guns. He had all the protection he needed in the twenty-four deputies who worked the Music Hall. At least that's the way he figured." She looked up at Liddell. "Why would they kill him, Johnny?"

Liddell shrugged his shoulders. "Story is someone's trying to sell the big boys protection. The longer they hold off paying, the higher the tab goes. Just to show he's not kidding he knocks off a couple of them—Adams and Fat Mike. That's the story."

"Do you believe it?"

"I don't know. Do you?"

The redhead shook her head. "No. I think he was killed because someone wanted something he had. He probably figured something like that, too. That's why he sent for you."

"Could be."

The redhead got up from the couch, walked over to Liddell. "Where does that leave me?"

Liddell's eyes took appreciative inventory of the red-head's assets. "You don't need him any more, baby. You can make it on your own, with no strings, no obliga-tions. This could be a good break for you."

The redhead shook her head. "I don't mean that. I mean if they killed him for some other reason." She licked at her lips. "They knew I was his girl. Maybe they'll think I know too much." She put her hand on his arm. "I'm scared."

"You're not the only one, baby. Benny Lewine and Eddie Morrow were making like castanets with their teeth." He squinted thoughtfully. "If they're right and a shake artist is behind this, you've got nothing to worry about."

"But if it's what I think?"

"We'll just have to nail the killer before he gets any more ideas."

The redhead shuddered involuntarily. Some of the color had drained from her face. "Don't let anything happen to me, Johnny." She shook her head from side to side. "I wish I'd never gotten mixed up with them. They're like mad dogs. They don't care who they kill."

"You should have thought of that before. Everything has a price tag. People who can't afford to buy shouldn't go window shopping."

"It's too late now. I'm in too deep. What should I do?"

Liddell shrugged. "You mean you've got a choice? We stand pat and leave the next move up to them. If they keep leading, they may make a mistake. Any change in plans? The opening going on as planned tomorrow night?"

The redhead nodded.

"Good. Act as if nothing happened. As far as you know, Fat Mike is alive and well. You don't know anything about his business, you don't want to know anything. You haven't seen him since you got back from New York, you spent all your time making plans for the opening."

"I understand." Lee Loomis laid her hand on his arm. "Where can I reach you if I need you?"

"I'm in 1D in Bungalow 8. The far side of the pool. If I'm not there, have me paged. I'll try to stay close."

The redhead worked at a smile, almost made it.

SEVEN

Bungalow 8 was a dormitory-type building with two stories of one-room accommodations. It was set back near the parking lot, protected from a view of the lot by thick, lush foliage; protected within from the sound of the lot's operations by soundproofing.

Liddell headed for the entrance of Bungalow 8 with visions of a cool shower and a change of clothes before dinner. Beyond the entrance a cream-colored Cadillac was drawn up to the curb.

As Liddell reached the steps leading into his bungalow, the front right door of the Cadillac swung open, the man named Whitey stepped out.

"Just a second," he called to Liddell.

Johnny grimaced, waited until the man had sauntered up to him. "You didn't have to go to all this trouble to make me feel at home," Liddell told him. "I would have found my own way."

"Very funny," Whitey acknowledged dryly. "We've been waiting for you, shamus."

"The name is Liddell."

Whitey continued to chew on the everpresent toothpick. "That so?" He smiled around the toothpick. "Always nice to meet an important guy." He eyed Liddell coolly. "And you must be a real important guy."

"How's that?"

Whitey made a production out of a shrug. "Real modest, too." He tugged the toothpick from between his teeth, flipped it into the grass. "First Mr. Klein sends all the way to New York for you." He bobbed his head in deference. "Now Mr. Sommers looks all over for you. He wants to see you so bad, he tells me not to come back without you."

Liddell shrugged. "He just wasn't looking in the right places."

"He still wants to see you. Real bad."

"Where?"

"I'll take you there." He nodded to the car. "All the comforts of home. Air conditioned and all." He walked back to the car, stood alongside the open door. "We can all sit up front. It's pal-ier that way."

Liddell ambled back to where the car stood, recognized the deputy who had driven him to the Las Palmas Arms. He greeted him, slid in alongside him. Whitey slid on the outside, pulled the door shut. "Okay, Tommy. Let's go." ·

"Where did you say we were meeting Sommers?" Liddell asked.

"I didn't."

The car purred smoothly out of the driveway, merged with the westbound stream of traffic. Just beyond the far end of the Strip, darkness seemed to close in on the car like a cloud. The driver snapped on his lights, the twin beams sliced paths through the rapidly spreading dusk that turns the desert from a rosy hue to a deep purple in minutes.

Liddell settled back, found a cigarette, lit it. On one side, the deputy was giving all his attention to the big

50

car. On the other, Whitey sat slumped down in his seat, his hat tilted over his eyes. Neither showed much inclination for talking.

The driver handled the car with the ease and skill of an experienced wheelman. About six miles out of town, Liddell became aware of a bright aura in the sky ahead. As they approached, the lighted area became brighter until at last it broke down into an emergency truck with its floodlights spotting a car parked at the side of the road. A group of other cars were parked near by, a small knot of men huddled around the car commanding all the attention.

The Cadillac eased to a stop behind the emergency truck, Whitey pushed the door open on his side. "You wait here," he snapped at Liddell. He got out of the car, walked over to the clot of men around the other car. After a moment, he was back. "You can go over now."

Liddell walked across to where the small group of men were staring into the front seat of the car impaled by the floodlights. He was able to make out the figure of a man sitting at the wheel, a gross figure of a man.

Martin Sommers waved him over to where he was standing with a man wearing a western type sheriff's fedora.

"We been trying to reach you, Liddell." There was an edge of irritation to his voice.

"You didn't tell me you wanted me to give you a timetable of where I'd be and when." He looked over to the car. "Fat Mike?"

Sommers nodded. "This is our sheriff, Liddell. Tom Regan. He's a good friend. When one of his boys investigated and found Mike, we were the first ones he notified."

Liddell acknowledged the introduction. "Any idea of how long he's been sitting there, sheriff?"

Regan shoved the fedora to the back of his head, scratched at the thick white mane. "Hard to say. Been pretty hot most of the day and the temperature inside that car must be at least 112. I'm no medical man but my guess is he's been in there most of the afternoon." He wrinkled his nose. "Don't keep too good in this kind of weather."

"How'd he get it?"

"Shot. Side of the head. Looks like he might have done it himself." A panel truck with red tinted headlights joined the group of cars parked near the death car. "That's the medical examiner's boys. I'll see you gents later."

Sommers waited until the sheriff was out of earshot. "You buy the suicide bit?"

Liddell shook his head. "A guy doesn't send for a private cop and pay him five grand to get him out of something and then do the dutch before the man even arrives." He shook his head. "Far's I can find out, he didn't even own a gun."

Sommers rubbed the heel of his hand along the side of his chin. "This is really going to stampede the boys. You think this is tied in with the Adams kill?"

"Different MO. Different weapon." Liddell said.

"They're both just as dead," Sommers muttered. He watched while the white-coated figures struggled with the stiffened figure behind the wheel. "Mike didn't believe in paying off. He wanted to fight. You know that?"

"How about you?"

The tall man shook his head. "A quarter of a million dollars is a lot of money," he grumbled. "But Mike still has his share and it's not about to do him any good, is it?"

"You tell the sheriff about the note and the phone calls?"

52

Sommers shook his head. "It'll work out better all around if he writes it off as suicide. It sure wouldn't look good for us if somebody up north got the idea we couldn't protect our own layouts."

The morgue attendants finally got the body from behind the wheel, laid it out on the stretcher. Johnny Liddell walked over, followed by the gambler.

Fat Mike was older and even heavier than the last time Liddell had seen him. Death had softened the hard lines of his mouth, had erased the menace that had always shone from beneath his heavily-veined lids.

He lay there in the merciless beam of the spotlight, eyes staring sightlessly at the sky. A dark hole in the right side of his face was diagonally above the ragged exit on the other side where the slug had torn away a piece of the jaw on its way out.

Sommers took a deep breath. "The heat and flies sure played hell with him, didn't they?"

"He wasn't much to look at to start with. It's a cinch this didn't improve him any."

Sommers dug a handkerchief from his hip pocket, held it to his lips. "I've had enough of this. I'm going back to town. Use a lift?"

Liddell looked around, nodded. "There's nothing we can do here. If there was any chance of finding any footprints anywhere near the car, that thundering herd has sure stamped them out."

Sommers seemed unconcerned, turned and headed for a black Imperial parked at the far edge of the parked cars. At the wheel was the tired-eyed man in the seersucker suit. He grinned at Liddell as Johnny and Martin Sommers stepped into the back seat, sank back against the cushions.

EIGHT

Johnny Liddell sat in one corner of the back seat of the limousine, Martin Sommers in the other, each occupied with his own thoughts. Liddell squirmed into a more comfortable position, looked up to the man in the seersucker suit on the other side of the glass partition that separated the two seats.

"That glass soundproof?" Liddell wanted to know.

Sommers started slightly, came out of his reverie. "The windshield between Farmer and us, you mean?" Liddell nodded. "Completely. He couldn't hear a gun go off back here. Why?"

"I've been thinking this whole thing over, Sommers. You're going to have a tough time making that suicide verdict stick." Liddell fumbled through his pockets, came up with a rumpled cigarette. "Even a hick sheriff should be able to figure from the angle the bullet took that—"

"Regan's no hick sheriff, Liddell, he's been around. And, as I told you, he's a good friend. We tell him not to tire his brain, he doesn't tire his brain." The gambler's face was a damp blur in the weak light of the match Liddell held to his cigarette. "He'll see to it that the medical examiner plays ball, too."

54

"And the guy who killed Fat Mike walks away from it?"

Sommers was silent for a moment. "Mike's dead. Nothing we can do can change that or bring him back. We let the word out that he's been murdered and all kinds of heat goes on. From the authorities, from the boys up north, from everybody. It goes down as suicide."

Liddell blew out a stream of smoke, watched the air conditioner suck it toward the vents. "Then you're going to pay off?"

"I don't think we have much choice." Sommers took the cigarette holder from his breast pocket, chewed on the end. "You heard the boys this afternoon after that phone call. You should have heard them when I called them to tell them the sheriff had found Mike's body. All they want is to get this monkey off their back."

"A million dollars is a lot of money. What kind of insurance are you getting that he won't be back for more?" .

Sommers shook his head. "We're not looking that far ahead. Nobody wants to take the chance of being next on the list." He sighed deeply. "I never considered myself a coward, Liddell, but I'm afraid I have to go along with them. No amount of money can do Mike Klein any good now."

"This boy couldn't have played his cards better. He's dealing with some of the most case-hardened characters in the business and he's got them shaking like a bunch of old maids."

"Because he's like a will of the wisp," Sommers complained. "Nobody knows who this guy is or anything about him."

Liddell stared out the window at the purple black of the desert, the darker masses of the mountains in the distance. "I wouldn't say that."

55

The man on the other side stared at him. "You got some ideas?"

Liddell looked over to him, wagged his head. "Nothing I could persuade the boys to hold off with," he conceded. "But a couple of things. He must be a guy who knows the boys, knows they've gotten a little soft."

Sommers thought about that. "That could be a matter of opinion."

"Okay. Will you buy this? He's got to be a guy who's close enough to the boys so they trust him?"

"Why?"

Liddell shrugged. "When you were looking for me, I was over at Fat Mike's bungalow. I took a good look around. There was no sign of a struggle, nothing out of place. So Fat Mike walked out under his own power." He stared at the dim blur of Sommers's face. "Right?"

"Maybe they grabbed him after he left his bungalow."

Liddell snorted. "He's got a baby army in that place. No one could put the snatch on him there." He shook his head. "And with what happened to Larry Adams fresh in his mind, he wouldn't be getting into any cars unless he knew damn well whose car he was getting into." He turned, stared out the window again. "The killer had to be someone he knew and trusted," he repeated.

"How about Larry Adams?"

Liddell shrugged. "How do we know what happened to Adams? You say he was murdered. For all you know or anybody knows, the killer was right there in the room with him, talking things over. One way or another, he gets behind him and that's it." He sniffed loudly. "You and your housebroken sheriff made it impossible for anyone to find out what actually did happen there. But in Fat Mike's case we don't have to guess. We know."

56

There was a worried note in Sommers's voice. "But who could be behind all this?"

"That's the jackpot question." Liddell chain-lit a fresh butt on the stub between .his fingers, crushed the old one out in the ash tray at his elbow. "How about Laughing Boy?"

"Laughing Boy?"

"The creep they call Whitey. He was close to Fat Mike, wasn't he?"

"Yeah, but you're out in left field, Liddell. Whitey's been with Fat Mike since the old days. He's been his right hand, Mike couldn't operate without Whitey."

"That's what I mean. Fat Mike is nothing without Whitey. Yet Mike rakes in millions operating the Music Hall and Whitey stands by and picks up the crumbs. You think maybe a character like this, mightn't decide it's about time to share the wealth?"

Sommers shook his head. "You didn't know their set-up. Whitey could have anything Mike had, they were that close."

"Yeah? How about the redhead, Mike's redhead? I saw Whitey look her over today. He wants a piece of that so bad he can taste it."

"Even if you're right, you think Whitey would pull a thing like this just for a dame? They're a dime a dozen out here, Liddell."

"Not only for the dame, Sommers. Whitey is number two man, he's always been number two man. You think anybody likes to stay a number two man all his life?" He shook his head, blew smoke at the air conditioning vent. "A lot of the boys in this town were number two men once—Rossi, Morrow, even Fat Mike himself. They got tired of holding the flashlight. What makes Whitey any different from them?" He nodded to the driver in the front seat. "Or your boy? Don't you think for once he'd like to know how it feels to be riding in the back seat, instead of—"

"Farmer?" Sommers snorted. "You're out of your mind. I'd stake my life on Farmer."

"It could be that's just what you're doing. Look, you think a guy like that appreciates it that you let him sit in the lobby and act like an airborne checkroom for anybody who comes to see you? You think maybe he doesn't start wondering why it's you upstairs and not him? It's only human nature."

Sommers frowned, shook his head. "I don't buy it." But he stared at the back of the driver's head thoughtfully, plucked at his nostrils with thumb and forefinger.

"You asked me who it could be. I'm not saying it was Whitey or Farmer, but it could be. Or it could be some of the younger punks that are tired of waiting for the older guys to die off and are speeding things up." He shrugged. "Maybe the note and the calls are just a blind so you'll be looking for a shakedown mob, instead of someone closer to home."

Sommers tapped the stem of the empty cigarette holder against his teeth, lapsed into silence. Then, "What was Mike's idea? Who did he think was behind this?"

Liddell shook his head. "I never talked to Mike."

The man alongside him turned, frowned. "Mike told us he had hired you to come out here and work on this for him."

"That's right."

"Well, he certainly didn't hire you by ouija board. He must have given you some idea of what he expected you to do for him."

"Mike didn't reach me. He had his babe, the redhead,

get in touch. She just told me that Mike thought Adams was murdered and wanted me to find the murderer."

Sommers snorted softly. "And you took the case on that basis?"

"There were a few inducements."

"Ten thousand dollars, for instance?"

Liddell grinned. "Among others."

Ahead of them the lights from the Strip sprayed a multicolored brilliance into the sky. Sommers turned, stared at it. "What are you planning to do now?"

Liddell shrugged. "Stay around for a while. Have a look around."

"Would you be willing to take care of the payoff for us when the time comes?"

"You're sure you're going through with it?"

Sommers paused. "That's what the boys want."

"And you?"

Sommers shook his head. "What I think doesn't matter. The way things are going, I may toss in my cards. I want to stay alive long enough to walk away." He looked over to Liddell. "Some of the boys can never leave Las Palmas. I can."

Liddell nodded. "I'll take care of the payoff for you."

The tanned man nodded his thanks, they both lapsed into silence.

Benny Lewine operated the Blue Fountain, a quarter of a mile down the Strip and on the opposite side of the highway from the Music Hall. From the road it was a sprawling salmon-colored modern pastel with a white-tile roof and trim. In front of the porte-cochere, a spectacular sign in the shape of a huge blue fountain spurted streams into the sky, dyed the highway a soft blue.

59

The Blue Fountain motif was continued in the Fountain Bar. The bar itself was circular, set in the center of the room. It had blue-leather elbow rests, matching stools. In the center of the bar a miniature fountain gurgled and spurted, its spray dyed by hidden blue lights. One whole side of the room was a picture window that looked out into the bottóm of the pool. When there were swimmers in it they gave the effect of being headless as they thrashed by, hands, legs and torsos undulating.

The room was dim, intimate. The only lighting aside from the fountain came from hidden fixtures in the corners. A number of comfortable armchairs and low tables were scattered around the room.

Johnny Liddell walked into the Fountain Bar, looked around. Only a few of the tables were occupied, a handful of people leaned against the bar. Most of the Blue Fountain's patrons were out in the casino hoping audibly that tonight they wouldn't lose more than they could afford.

Liddell walked over to a table near the wall, selected a chair that would give him a full view of the room. A waitress materialized out of the gloom, smiled tentatively. Her long legs were unencumbered by a brief pair of shorts, above she stretched a white peasant blouse to the limits of credibility.

"Benny Lewine around?" Liddell asked.

She gave no sign that she minded the inventory he took of her assets. "I imagine he's checking the buffet set-up."

"Tell him Johnny Liddell is out here. I'd like to talk to him."

She repeated the name Johnny Liddell, as though filing it for future notice. "Is there anything else you'd like?"

60

Liddell considered, sighed. "Yeah. But I guess I'll have to settle for a drink. Scotch on the rocks."

She smiled again, headed back across the room. Liddell settled back, lit up a cigarette.

He was on his second scotch and his third cigarette when Benny Lewine appeared in the entrance to the bar, squinted around. He recognized Liddell at the table near the wall, started toward him.

"You wanted to see me?" He breathed noisily through his broken nose.

Liddell indicated the chair opposite him. "I thought you'd want to hear about Fat Mike."

"Sommers already told me. So he's dead." He shrugged. "Nobody figures on living forever." He didn't quite bring it off.

"Just like that? One of your associates gets hit, so you write it off and do nothing about it? You must be real scared, Benny!"

Lewine shoved his battered face across the table, snarled, "I'm not scared, shamus. Of nobody or nothing. And don't forget it."

"You sure could fool me." Liddell picked up his glass, swirled the liquor around the side. "It takes a real scare to make a man talk about burying his friends instead of getting the guys who did it."

Lewine looked around, pulled the chair out, dropped into it. "Look, Liddell, Fat Mike brought you out here to do a job for him. Okay, so he's checked in, so you can get to keep the loot. But leave things alone for the rest of us." He leaned across the table, Liddell could smell the foulness of his breath. "We're paying off, we're walking away from it."

"You sound real broken up."

"Adams and Fat Mike are the ones who're broken up.

And nobody can put them together again. Me, I like it the way I am. It's my skin and I don't like walking around with holes in it." He started to get up. Liddell waved him back into his seat.

"You said something at the meeting that interested me, Benny. You were talking about the young punks that can't wait to get their share—"

Lewine wagged his head. "I don't know what you're talking about. All I know is a couple of my friends conked out. Larry Adams with a bum ticker. Fat Mike did the dutch because he was worried about his health."

"Who takes over their operation, Benny?"

"I don't know." He leaned across the table. "And if I were you, shamus, I wouldn't ask so many questions. A lot of people might figure you were getting real curious." He pushed back his chair, swung around.

Liddell could see the ex-pug's shoulders stiffen. He looked past him to the bar. A man was perched on one of the bar stools. He was in his early twenties, his long black hair slicked back at the sides, a mass of curls at the top. In the half light, his face was pitted and marked with acne. He hopped off the stool, took his time about crossing to where Liddell sat.

From close he gave off the expensive odor of Charbert. He twisted the corners of his thin lips up in what was intended to be a smile. "Just heard about Fat Mike." He looked from Lewine to Liddell and back, shook his head. "This climate sure is tough on older guys. Too much heat, you think?" He rolled his eyes to Liddell. "I don't think I know your friend."

"Liddell's my name. Johnny Liddell."

The man with the pitted face seemed to be trying to place the name, snapped his fingers. "You're the"—he seemed to be fumbling for a word—"the private dick from New York." He nodded as though impressed by his

62

own memory. "I've heard of you. I'm Carl Jensen. From Detroit."

"You operating down here?" Liddell asked.

Jensen smiled deprecatingly, shrugged. "Just a petty larceny layout. Nothing big like the big operators. I have a piece of a spot downtown, on Front Street. Joint called the Big Payoff." He shrugged again. "Strictly a nickel and dime operation." He looked around enviously. "Nothing like the big guys." His eyes finished a circuit of the room, stopped on Lewine. "Maybe one of these days I'll latch onto a bankroll and move up. Never can tell, eh?" He turned to Liddell, nodded. "Glad to meet you." He turned back to Lewine. "Tell the boys I was sorry to hear about Fat Mike. And so soon after Adams." He shook his head, then sauntered back to the bar.

"Young punk," Lewine muttered half under his breath. "Goddam young punk!"

"Sounds like an enterprising young man to me," Liddell commented.

Lewine whirled around, leaned over the table. "He muscled in on that nickel and dime operation downtown. He thinks he can pull the same muscle around here, he's crazy."

"Maybe he's not going to need muscle. Like he says, maybe he'll come up with a bankroll."

"Who's going to give a punk like that a bankroll?"

Liddell grinned bleakly. "Maybe you—and the rest of the boys."

Lewine's jaw sagged. He stared at Liddell for a moment, shook his head. "He wouldn't have the guts."

"There's one way to find out. Don't make the payoff. Let the shake artist try another move."

The lumps of scar tissue he had for brows half veiled the former lightweight's eyes. He twisted his scrambled features into a scowl. "I told you, shamus, we're walking away from the whole thing. Nobody wants any trouble, and we don't want you starting any." He straightened up. He turned in time to see the young hood walking out of the bar. "We'll go along this time. But there better not be a next time."

NINE

Sheriff Tom Regan had a cubbyhole office on the ground floor of the County Courthouse which housed the Las Palmas Police Department.

Johnny Liddell followed one of the meandering walks that trisected the memorial park in front of the courthouse. In the center of the park, the equestrian statue of General Sherman showed signs of losing an aerial battle with the pigeons.

The street lamps that lined the walk spilled yellow pools of light down over their bases, and drained away into the shadows. Here and there a bench was occupied: those closer to the light by older citizens who had neither the means nor the inclination to go up against the wheels and the slots on the Strip; those farther from the light occupied by couples who had the inclination—but it had nothing to do with the wheels or slots.

Johnny Liddell walked into the old building, headed to the rear of the hall where a frosted glass door proclaimed *Sheriff's Office*. He knocked, a gruff voice told him to come in.

Tom Regan sat at his desk, cards spread out for a game of solitaire. He glanced up as Liddell walked in, grunted as he recognized him, peeled three cards off the pack in his hand. He checked the black nine he turned up against each of the seven stacks in front of him, found no place to match it.

"Come in and close the door," he told Liddell without looking up.

Liddell walked in while the sheriff lifted the corners of each of the piles faced down, finally found the red ten he needed. He slipped out the red ten, laid it on a black Jack with a triumphant grin. "Damned if I don't think I'm going to make it."

"The way you play, how can you miss?" Liddell observed.

The white-haired man tossed the rest of the cards on the top of the desk, leaned back. "You been in this town long enough, you'll find out that's the only way there is to play. To win." He nodded to a chair alongside the desk. "Sit down."

Liddell pulled the chair up, dropped into it. "How'd you make out with Fat Mike?"

Regan shrugged. "Suicide all right. Doc says Mike was complaining of bad pains in his stomach last couple of weeks. Guess he thought it was something bad. You know?"

"How about the gun?" Liddell brought a pack of cigarettes from his pocket, shook one loose. He was about to return the pack to his pocket when the sheriff reached over, caught his wrist.

"Don't mind if I do."

"Be my guest." Liddell waited until the sheriff had stuck the cigarette in the corner of his mouth. "Use a light?"

The white-haired man nodded.

Liddell lit his from the same match, snapped it out.

66

"We were talking about the gun. Any chance of tracing it?"

Regan raised his eyebrows. "Tracing it? We don't have to. It was Mike's gun. Had a license for it in his name, in fact."

Liddell stopped with the cigarette halfway from his mouth. "You sure?"

"Should be. I issued the license myself." Regan pulled himself up from his chair, walked over to a filing cabinet, flipped through it, brought back a file. "The whole works." He opened the file, brought out a flimsy. "Statement from the doc that Mike thought he was a very sick man." He brought out another flimsy. "Medical examiner's office. Verdict to be posted is suicide." He flipped that back, picked up a small typewritten form. "Duplicate of the gun license. Number checks out with the gun." He snapped the folder closed. "Open and shut."

"Yes, isn't it?" Liddell snorted. "I suppose Fat Mike wanted to be cremated, too?"

Regan looked surprised. "Now what ever gave you that idea?" He shook his head. "No, sir. Mike will be buried in the Las Palmas cemetery. Just like he wanted. Matter of fact, they're getting him ready right now at the mortuary."

Liddell stared. "The body's been released for embalming already?"

Regan shrugged. He picked up the folder, returned it to the file. "We do things a lot faster hereabouts. They don't keep too good. The climate." He walked back to his chair, dropped into it. "Besides, he was in a pretty bad shape when we picked him up. No sense in delaying."

"What would you say if I said Mike was murdered?"

67

The sheriff sighed. "I'd say you were wrong. Two ways. One, he was a suicide. Two, you'd be starting a lot of unnecessary trouble that would make a lot of people unhappy. That wouldn't be smart, at all."

Liddell took the cigarette from between his lips, tapped a thin collar of ash from the end. "Mike sent for me. He thought Larry Adams was murdered."

The man behind the desk raised his eyebrows. "That so? Only goes to bear out what the doc said. Imagining things."

"I don't think he was."

"Of course he wasn't. Larry Adams died of a heart attack. Got a medical report that proves it."

"I don't mean that. I mean I don't think Fat Mike was imagining things. If he was, he has a lot of company in this town. There are a lot of people who think Larry Adams was murdered."

"That so?" Regan asked politely. "For instance?"

"Benny Lewine at the Blue Fountain. Eddie Morrow at the Cash Box. Al Rossi. Marty Sommers. They don't think it was a heart attack. And they don't think Fat Mike did the dutch."

Regan stared at him for a moment, pulled the telephone to the edge of the desk. He dialed a number, waited.

"Mr. Sommers? Sheriff Regan."

A man's voice was on the other end, the resonant kind which a telephone seems to make louder. A lawyer's voice.

"Everything's fine here," the sheriff assured him. "Just like we thought. Suicide. That is"—he looked over at Liddell—"I thought you agreed with me until this friend of yours came in. This Liddell fellow."

The voice on the other end sounded querulous, sharp.

The sheriff shrugged. "He seems to think you and some of the other operators aren't satisfied with the coroner's verdict. Now, if you want me to—"

The deep voice on the other end bellowed, the sheriff nodded his head. "That's what I thought. Only I wouldn't want there to be any questions in anybody's mind." He dropped the receiver on its hook, peered at Liddell.

"I don't know what you're selling, mister," he told Liddell mildly. "But we're not buying. Sounds to me like you're just out to stir up some trouble. Maybe pick yourself up some easy change." He shook his head. "You're in the wrong town." He checked his watch. "There's a nonstop flight to New York at ten in the morning. Why don't you be on it?"

"You running me out of town, Sheriff?"

Regan looked hurt. "Why you so set on taking the wrong attitude? It was just a suggestion, not an order." He took the butt from between his lips, crushed it out in the ash tray. "I'm only suggesting it for your own good. Man like you, acting like a bull in a china shop, could get hurt."

"It's been tried."

The white-haired man leaned back. "I can imagine. But if you insist on staying around town, let me give you some advice. You have no standing around here, official or unofficial." He raised his hand, cut Liddell off. "I know you've got a license. But you've got no client. Far's we're concerned you're just some outsider looking for trouble. You get out of line and you're likely to get stamped flat."

"And trying to find out who killed Fat Mike would be getting out of line?"

The sheriff looked pained again. "There you go again,

talking crazy. We know who killed Mike. He did, himself." He sighed. "I wish you'd decide to be on that plane in the morning. Take my advice and don't start anything you can't finish."

Liddell considered, nodded. "I guess that is pretty good advice, Sheriff," he conceded.

The man behind the desk grinned triumphantly. "Now you're acting smart like they said you were. I can get you a seat—"

"I didn't say I was leaving, Sheriff." Liddell got up, crushed out his butt in the sheriff's ash tray. "I'll be around for a while."

An ugly red flush started up the sheriff's neck from his collar. "You just said—"

"I said I was taking your advice. About not starting anything I couldn't finish." He walked to the door, stopped with his hand on the knob. "So I'll make sure to do just that. I'll finish anything I start." He walked out, slammed the door behind him.

The Big Payoff, Carl Jensen's gambling layout, was on Front Street, in downtown Las Palmas. Johnny Liddell left the County Courthouse, walked three blocks south, turned into a two-block stretch that was lined on either side by two- and three-story high neons advertising 21 parlors and roulette; a burlesque house that ground until 4 a.m., two pawnshops, a couple of small time night clubs and some nondescript bars.

At all hours of the day and night, the tide of pedestrians ebbs and flows along the length of Front Street. The stretch bears no more resemblance in population or appearance to the Strip than the Bowery does to Broadway in New York.

Johnny Liddell ambled down the block to the far cor-

70

ner. Here a two-story replica of a slot machine flashed on and off, spilling its colored jackpot from a neon maw, marking the entrance to the Big Payoff.

By contrast to the people on the Strip, the regulars along Front Street were shabby. But on their faces was the same fixed expression, the same breathless impatience to feed as much of their money into the machines as time would allow. On the Strip they rocketed from casino to casino in convertibles, here they shouldered their way through the crowds. But both were in a hurry to get some action.

Johnny Liddell walked past the honky-tonks that spilled loud and raucous music out onto the sidewalk, looked into the dim interiors where couples were locked in dances done with feet pasted to the same spot on the floor. Here and there a few drunks sat in doorways, oblivious to the cars lined up in hopeless traffic jams in the narrow street, drivers leaning on their horns, tempers fraying.

Liddell pushed his way into the Big Payoff. It was housed in the corner building, had been enlarged by knocking out the walls of four adjacent stores. The ceiling, two stories overhead, was decorated with old-fashioned crystal chandeliers that had been converted from gas to electricity at the turn of the century on the Barbary Coast, had worked their way to Las Palmas with all the other rejects.

A large oval bar had been built around a small bandstand where a trio was competing bravely with the rumble of conversation, the whir of the slot machines and the buzz of excitement from the roulette wheels. The bar itself was an ornate hangover from the nineties, featured heavily carved figures holding it up at either end. The backbar was made up of oversized, soaped mirrors,

71

topped by a large painting of a reclining overweight nymph.

One large area had been given over to the slots and it gave the appearance of some huge assembly line as the players automatically and uniformly pulled the upright levers, waited until the wheels stopped whirling, repeated the process with deadpan concentration.

The stools set in semicircles around the 21 tables were all filled, a voice over the loud speaker warned that the Payoff Bingo game was about to start. In the rear, a large wheel with its leather indicator stuttering from nail to nail drew a howl as it stopped on 82 and the lucky ones with their quarters on square 82 were being paid off at the rate of 20 to 1.

At the far side of the bar, the roulette wheels were marked by clusters of housewives, men in rough denims from near-by farms and ranches, an occasional group of sailors on furlough from San Diego. All over the room, the players were playing with fierce concentration. On the Strip they gambled with feverish gaiety, but on Front Street gambling was a serious matter. Here the machines fattened on grocery money, not the savings from some housewife's teapot put aside for vacations.

Johnny Liddell walked up to a man in a gray uniform, badge on his chest, everpresent .45 on his hip. "I'm looking for Carl Jensen. Is he around?"

The guard looked him over, turned and indicated a large boxlike structure built against the back wall in the center. It protruded out from the wall for several feet like a blockhouse.

"He's up in the office." He caught Liddell's sleeve as Johnny started to turn away. "You'll have to get an okay." He nodded to a booth where two men were making change. "There's a phone in the booth."

Liddell walked over to the booth, waited until the man behind the counter finished counting out twenty quarters for a five.

"I want to talk to Jensen. Guard said I could use your phone."

The man behind the counter nodded, dug under the counter, brought up a phone, put it to the side. "Dial three." He turned his interest to a middle-aged woman who was laboriously counting the nickels, dimes and pennies. She finally looked up triumphantly. "Seventy-five cents. That's three quarters." The man behind the counter scooped the money into his drawer, dropped three quarters.

"Must be having a good night, Rose," he said. "You walked out here flat a couple hours ago."

The woman grinned at him. "My luck's changed. I feel a jackpot coming." She scooped up the quarters, pushed her way through the others surrounding the booth, headed for the quarter slots.

Liddell dialed three, a heavy voice answered at the other end. "I want to talk to Carl Jensen. Tell him it's Liddell. I met him at the Blue Fountain tonight."

There was a pause, then the voice told him to stay where he was.

Liddell dropped the receiver on the hook, waited.

A man in the gray uniform of a guard shouldered his way through the crowd to where Liddell was standing. "You the guy wants to see Jensen?"

Liddell nodded.

The guard indicated that Johnny follow him, led the way past the bar to the fortlike structure. He stopped, rapped on a heavy metal door with his knuckles. A trap door slid open, a pair of eyes moved from the guard to Liddell and back.

"It's okay, Moe. Jensen wants to see him."

The trap door slid shut, the door opened wide enough for one man to pass through. As soon as he had stepped in, the door slid shut behind him.

Inside, a heavy-shouldered man with a shoulder holster strapped under his arm looked him over. "Up those stairs," he grunted. He didn't wait to see if Liddell followed his instructions, walked over to a wooden chair under an unshaded bulb, picked up a fact detective magazine and made himself comfortable.

Liddell climbed the iron-rung ladder to the upper story. It came out in a cleared space where three men sat at bulletproof windows which gave them an unhampered view of the floor below. Each man cradled an automatic shotgun under his arm. From here the three of them could cover the entire casino.

Jensen stood at the door in the rear of the blockhouse. He nodded to Liddell, motioned him in. Beyond there was a small office where several men punched adding machines, checking the totals against tapes they held in their hands. At the far side of the windowless room an automatic coin counter was counting the contents of canvas bags being fed into them by a patently bored attendant. Nearby another machine was counting and wrapping stacks of bills.

"Didn't figure on seeing you again so soon, Liddell." Jensen smiled. "What's on your mind?"

Johnny looked around, nodded. "Quite a set-up."

The man with the pitted face still grinned. "My contribution." He flattened the hair over his ears with the palm of his hand. "Used to be this place got knocked over by stickups two, three, maybe four times a year. There hasn't been a try made since I took over a piece."

"Quite a coincidence."

"Wasn't it?" Jensen led the way to a vacant desk with a chair facing it. "You didn't come to rubberneck. You didn't come to slum. So, like you got something on your mind, why don't we talk?"

"I just came from the sheriff's office."

Jensen laughed. "That clown! He couldn't locate a fat man in a phone booth."

"You don't think much of him?"

"All he's good for is to see nobody bothers the big operators. He uses his badge to make it legal if he leans too hard." He picked up a scimitar-shaped letter opener from the desk, dug at his nails. "What'd you and he have to talk about?"

Liddell shrugged. "A little of this, a little of that. I get the impression he'd like to see me out of town."

Jensen worked on his nails. "Figures. He's got this town eating out of his hand. He don't want any out-siders coming in lousing things up." He looked at Liddell. "One thing he does do good. That's keep the lid on. The big operators don't like things getting out of hand."

"Easy way to earn his keep."

The thin lips twisted upward in a grin. "This town was just made to get taken. A lot of drifters figure it for a soft touch. They bounce a little rubber, sometimes they gaff a bill or slip in some educated dice. One ambitious guy even tried to get by with a sleeve holdout. When they get caught, and they do, the operators turn them over to Regan. It's his job to convince them not to come back." He grinned sadistically. "He's an expert at it."

"I detected the warm breath of hospitality the minute I hit town," Liddell said.

"So why hang around? Fat Mike sent for you, but—" He broke off, laughed at the unasked question on Liddell's lips. "Word gets around. The boys in this town are allergic to the law. Even a private cop gets passed around the minute he shows."

"Sing Sing wireless."

"A lot of the boys got a warm feeling for Sing Sing." Jensen went back to work on his nails with the opener. "Like I was saying, Fat Mike sends for you. He does the dutch, so you couldn't have done him good." He looked up, squinted. "So what's to hang around for?"

"You sure Mike killed himself?"

"He sure didn't die of old age." The squint turned into a puzzled frown. "You got something to say, maybe we could stop waltzing around. You tell me what's on your mind, maybe I got some answers." He tossed the letter opener on the desk. "You sound like maybe you think Fat Mike got hit in the head."

Liddell shrugged. "Like you said, he didn't die from old age."

Jensen pursed his lips. "And the sheriff would cover, huh? It could be."

"Benny Lewine is scared of you, Jensen. Why?"

The dark-haired man grinned. "He don't like me hanging around his joint. He's got it figured I'm thinking of what changes I'm going to make when I take it over."

"And are you?"

A cold mask seemed to slip over Jensen's eyes. "If it wasn't for the way the sheriff backstops him, I would have done it long ago. He's aching to be taken."

"And what would Benny be doing all this time?"

The dark-haired man snorted. "He's old. And soft. Maybe he was a big man once. Now he's just a fat slob." He studied Liddell coldly. "Maybe that's what you're doing here. Maybe Benny figured you could throw some muscle around." He pasted a grin on his lips that failed to defrost his eyes. "You go back and tell him—"

"Tell him yourself. You were right the first time. I

came here to work for Fat Mike. He thought Larry Adams was murdered—" He tried to read the expression on the other man's face. "Or maybe that doesn't come as a surprise to you?"

The man behind the desk investigated the acne scars that pitted his cheek with the tips of his fingers, leaving them an angry red. "You leveling?"

Liddell nodded.

Jensen got up, paced behind the desk, his hands on his hips. "You say Fat Mike thought Adams was hit, and now you tell me Fat Mike got it, too." He stopped pacing, leaned across the desk. "You wouldn't be reading me a fairy tale, would you, Dad?"

"Why should I?"

Jensen considered it. He straightened up, flattened his hair over his ears. He finally nodded. "That's right. Why should you?"

"That leaves two spots with no front—"

The other man dropped into his desk chair, shook his head. "Word's already out. Whitey takes over at the Music Hall. There's a guy from Chicago already in line for Adams's spot." He laced his hands at the back of his neck, tilted his head up, stared at the ceiling. "Word would have to come from real high to okay a hit on big operators like that."

"The boys up north don't know they were killed. The sheriff saw to that."

The eyes rolled down from the ceiling, fixed on Liddell's face. "You're sure of that?"

Liddell nodded.

"That's very interesting."

"Mean something to you?"

Jensen pursed his lips, nodded slowly. "It could, Dad, it could." He grinned slowly. "Adams and Mike·Klein both killed and the boys up north don't know a thing about it. A man could add two and two and get some fancy figures out of that."

"Like how much?"

The grin on Jensen's face broadened. "Like a man could get to be a millionaire overnight."

TEN

It was after one by the time Johnny Liddell finally headed back to his room. He could only hope that by stirring up some activity the killer would be forced to show his hand. The more times he went to the well, the bigger the chance he'd make a mistake. It could be wearing on the rest of the operators, Liddell admitted to himself glumly, especially if the killer needed several dry runs before he got careless.

This time he got beyond the steps leading to the bungalow, headed down the hall to his door. He inserted his key in the lock, pushed the door open, frowned when he saw the room was in complete darkness, the heavy drapes blotting out the windows.

He stepped in, fumbled for the light switch.

The arm that slipped around his throat in a mugger's grip almost cut off his wind entirely. He felt the snout of a gun jabbed into his back just above the belt. He offered no further resistance.

"Let's have some light," a voice grated close to his ear.

The table lamp snapped on, spilling yellow light into the room. Lee Loomis was sitting in the chair near the table, facing the door, she held a .38 in her hand. She stared at Liddell, signaled to the man behind him.

The pressure was released from his throat, Liddell sucked in a deep breath. "What is this?" he managed to croak.

"Sorry, Johnny," the redhead told him. "We couldn't be sure it was you."

"Who'd you think it was? Fat Mike?" He spun on the man behind him, recognized him as the deputy named Thompson who had been at the office with Whitey earlier. "What's he doing here?"

The redhead got up from the chair, walked over to Liddell. "We were only trying to warn you."

"Warn me about what?" His eyes jumped from Lee to the deputy. "That I ought to get out of town? That seems to be a civic project around here."

The deputy returned his .45 to its holster. "I was going off duty about an hour ago. As I passed the registration desk, I heard some friends of yours asking for you. The fag behind the desk checked your room by phone, told them you were out. They left a message for you." He dug into his tunic pocket. "I was curious, so I checked."

He handed Liddell a folded envelope. On the face of it was scrawled *Johnny Liddell*. He pulled out a piece of notepaper, turned it over, looked up. "Blank."

The deputy nodded. "It's an old trick. They wanted to know what room you were in. The clerk drops the message in your box and they know. I figured you were about to have some visitors." He shrugged. "I couldn't find you, so I figured maybe Miss Loomis might know where you were."

"Why?"

"To tip you off."

Liddell continued to stare at him. "Why?"

"It's against the policy of the house to have corpses cluttering up our deluxe rooms," Thompson snarled. He turned, reached for the doorknob.

"Wait a minute, Tommy," the redhead urged. She turned to Liddell. "Tommy isn't like the rest of these deputized goons, Johnny. He was a New York cop and a good one before he got sick. He figured you were in a tough spot and he wanted to help."

Liddell didn't take his eyes off the deputy. "What gave him the idea I was in a tough spot? Maybe they were friends of mine."

The deputy looked from Liddell to the girl and back. "In the first place, I'm not since yesterday. I can smell a button a mile off. And if these characters were friends, you don't need enemies." He hooked his thumbs in his gunbelt.

"So you decided to draw cards in the game. It don't make sense."

"To me it does," the deputy drawled. "Fat Mike was a meatball, sure. But I knew him since we were kids. When I got sick, he picked up the hot for me. When I was well enough he gave me a job." He scowled at Liddell. "He was enough sold on you to bring you out on a job. That's good enough for me."

Liddell stared for a moment, nodded. "Okay, so I owe you an apology."

"You don't owe me a thing." He studied Liddell's face for a moment. "I just want you to level with me on one thing. Word is that Mike did the dutch. Did he?"

Liddell walked over to his bag, snapped open the catches looked up. "Not in my book." He brought a bottle of scotch out. "The verdict is suicide, but nobody but a contortionist could have shot himself the way he was shot." He ripped the foil off the bottle. "The bullet

81

went in higher than it came out. Either the killer was standing over him, or Mike's head was pulled back against the cushion when he got it." He turned to the redhead. "You told me he didn't own a gun?"

The redhead nodded. "He was deathly afraid of them." She turned to the deputy for corroboration. "Isn't that right, Tommy?"

"I never saw him with one. I never knew of him having one," Thompson told her. "Even back in the old days in New York he never carried one. He used his hands for persuaders. Like I said, he was a meatball, not a button."

"Funny thing," Liddell said. "The sheriff has a copy of the gun permit issued to Fat Mike. All signed, sealed and real legal like." He walked into the bathroom, came out with two glasses wrapped in cellophane. There was another glass with the carafe on the night table. "How about a drink? Just to show there's no hard feelings?"

The deputy nodded his head. "No hard feelings."

Liddell tore the cellophane off two of the glasses, spilled some scotch into them. He softened it with water from the carafe, handed one to the redhead, the other to the deputy. He poured himself a drink in the third glass.

He stopped with the glass halfway to his lips, frowned. The sound of a key being fitted into the lock was unmistakable. He indicated for the deputy to step back, douse the lights. There was a faint click as the room dissolved into darkness.

Liddell caught the redhead by the arm, pushed her toward the bathroom door. The only sound in the room was the sound of loud breathing. His own. He tugged his .45 from its holster, waited.

Slowly the hall door inched open, a long finger of dim light from the hallway probed into the room. It widened

82

into a triangle, was temporarily blotted out as a figure inched into the room, closed the door after him.

There was a scratching noise as the man's hand felt along the wall for the light switch. Suddenly, the lights flashed on.

Liddell had the impression of a tall, heavy-shouldered man. A .38 looked dwarfed in his hamlike fist. The man stood frozen, almost in suspended animation. He took in the situation at a glance, pumped a bullet as Thompson moved in on him. The slug caught the deputy, spun him half around, sent him staggering back. A chair tangled with his legs, spilled him onto the floor. The man with the gun tried to swing on Liddell.

The .45 in Johnny's hand roared twice. The noise was deafening in the soundproofed room. The heavy slugs hit the big man, lifted him off the floor and slammed him back against the door, where he slid to a sitting position. He tried to lift his gun to fire, but it had suddenly become too heavy. Little beads of sweat popped on the man's forehead as he struggled. Finally, he dropped his gun, laced his hands across his mid-section in a futile attempt to stem the flow of red that was already beginning to seep through his fingers.

The bathroom door flew open. "You all right, Johnny?" the redhead gasped.

"Bring a couple of towels. Thompson caught one," Liddell told her. He walked over to where the deputy was struggling to pull himself to a sitting position. Liddell helped him up, braced his back against the wall. He tore open the deputy's tunic, grunted, fingered a deep dent in the deputy's shield. "Take a look. This took the slug and deflected it. All he's got is a sore chest and the wind knocked out of him."

The deputy sucked a lungful of air, winced. Liddell pressed his fingers gently around the bruised area, shook his head. "No bones broken. Maybe a bit stiff in that wing for a few days, though."

The redhead fought a losing battle to keep her eyes off the dead man. "How about him?"

Liddell shook his head. "He won't be giving anybody any more trouble. Not wearing a .45 slug for a belt buckle like he is."

Thompson reached up, caught Liddell's arm, pulled himself to his feet. He stood swaying for a moment until he got his balance. "That damn slug had the kick of a mule," he grunted. He staggered over to the dead man, studied him. "This is one of them," he looked at Liddell. "He had a partner working with him. He must be hanging around outside some place."

Liddell walked over, put the sole of his foot against the dead man's shoulder, toppled him out of the way. He opened the door a crack, satisfied himself that the corridor was empty.

"If he heard those shots—"

The deputy shook his head. "They soundproof these rooms real good. They don't want anything interfering with the marks' sleep. They want them nice and fresh for the tables." He buttoned his tunic. "Suppose I have a look around? I know what the other guy looks like and he won't get the wind up seeing one of the employees making the rounds."

"If you feel up to it."

Thompson adjusted his tie, flattened his hair with the palm of his hand. "I'll rap three times. If anybody tries coming in without rapping, start blasting. It'll be his buddy come looking for him."

Liddell nodded, opened the door wide enough for the deputy to slip through. Much of the color had drained from the redhead's face, leaving her lipstick and eye shadow as dark smears against the pallor.

"How about that drink we never had time ₊to finish?" Liddell suggested. He picked up the glass where the redhead had set it down untouched, added more scotch to it and handed it to her. He waited until she had taken a big swallow before he picked his up. Her eyes watered, she took another swallow.

"What about him?" Her eyes persisted on returning to the dead man.

"If he wants a drink, let him get it himself."

"Johnny, I'm serious. What are you going to do with him? You can't leave him here. And if you try to get him out—"

She was interrupted by three sharp taps on the door.

Liddell tugged the .45 from its holster, walked over to the door, opened it a crack, the snout of the .45 at the opening. The deputy stood in the corridor. Liddell opened the door to let him in.

Thompson nodded. "They had it all nice and pat. Guess what they have pulled up right in back of the bungalow?" He grinned bleakly. "The pickup wagon for the medical examiner's office. All nice and neat. Junior here picks you off, they take you out the back way, give you a free ride to the county morgue." He shrugged. "What could be cleaner?"

Liddell walked over to the bureau, brought the deputy a drink. "That could work two ways." He dropped his eyes thoughtfully to the dead man. "Think they'd mind if we borrowed their rig for a little while?"

"But there's another one out there, Tommy says," the redhead protested.

"You see him, Tommy?"

The deputy took a deep swallow from his glass, nodded. "He's having himself a smoke. He's standing at the back of the truck. Near the rear exit to the bungalow."

Liddell finished his glass, set it down. "So, if I go out the front door and work my way around, I'd be coming up behind him. Right?"

The deputy considered. "You might," he told him cautiously.

"You see that Lee gets back to her bungalow, Tommy. I'll handle it from here."

The redhead shook her head. "You're going to need help, Johnny. You can't handle it all alone." She dug the .38 out of her bag. "I can get back to my bungalow. You stay and help him, Tommy," she told the deputy.

"She's right. If you're figuring on doing what I think you're figuring on, you'll never make it. Not alone," the deputy chimed in. "I'll take her as far as the pool, clear of the bungalow area. Then I'm coming back."

Liddell shrugged. "I'm not going to argue. All contributions gratefully received." He checked the corridor again, nodded to Thompson and the redhead that the coast was clear. They slipped out, headed down the deserted corridor.

As soon as they had reached the front door, Liddell stepped out, closed his door behind him. He walked slowly to the door at the far end. When he stepped out, he could see Lee and Thompson heading down the incline toward the pool area.

He turned, walked in the opposite direction to the far end of the bungalow. Behind him, the casino spilled yellow light out onto the terrace and reflected goldenly from the water in the pool. Bungalow 8 gave no signs of occupancy, the windows heavily shrouded with thick drapes. Only the entrance behind him showed light.

At the end of the building, he swung right, headed for the rear. Here there was no light at all. Slowly, carefully, he picked his way to the rear. He flattened himself against the building, stuck an eye around the corner.

Dimly outlined, he could make out the bulk of the pickup truck, the red blinker casing on top glinting dully. He waited until his eyes became accustomed to the gloom. At the rear of the truck he could see a pinpoint of blood-red light that glowed and brightened, then died away. As he watched the red dot described an arc, hit the building with a force that sent sparks scattering. After a moment there was a weak light. Liddell got a faint impression of a man's face as the match was held to a fresh cigarette.

The outside man was showing signs of getting impatient.

Liddell pulled up his lapels, covered his white shirt, started cautiously across from the end of the building to the big hedge that separated it from the parking lot. After what seemed an eternity, he melted into the shadows. Flattening out against the hedge, he worked his way down slowly until he was opposite the mortuary truck.

With its bulk between him and the second gunman, Liddell crossed to the truck. He stooped down, crept around its radiator, came up behind the other man. He tugged the .45 from its holster, peered around at where the man stood watching the rear entrance to the building.

"Okay, buddy. One move out of you and this is Cinderella's coach, only midnight's never coming."

The gunman stiffened, started to turn, decided against it.

Liddell came up behind him, jabbed the .45 in his back. He reached into the man's jacket pocket, brought out a .38.

"You're making a mistake, friend. This is official business. Now, before you get into trouble—" He started to turn around.

Liddell laid the barrel of the .45 across the side of his

head, the man unbent at the knees, went down. He was on hands and knees, shaking his head, when Liddell brought the barrel down on the top of his head. It slammed his face into the dirt, he didn't move.

Liddell reached up, opened the rear doors to the truck. There were two stretchers in their racks. He caught the unconscious man under the arms, lifted him into the truck. He laid him out on one of the stretchers, strapped him on. As an afterthought, he covered him with a rough piece of canvas. He stepped outside, filled his lungs with air. It tasted good after the heavy smell of death that permeated the interior of the truck.

He lit a cigarette, took two deep drags to cleanse his mouth and nostrils of the smell. Then he dropped the cigarette to the ground, crushed it out and started up the back entrance into Bungalow 8.

The doorway to 1D was almost diagonally across from the rear exit to the building. He crossed the hall to his door, rapped three times. After a moment, the door was opened a crack. When Thompson recognized him, he pulled it all the way open. Johnny walked in.

"Okay?" the deputy wanted to know.

Liddell nodded. "We have deluxe accommodations for our friend here. Not air conditioned, maybe, but he doesn't look the particular type."

"What about his buddy?"

"He got tired and laid down: I covered him with a blanket. It gets real chilly out here in the desert at night." Liddell reached over, caught the dead man by the arms, started to lift him to his feet.

"Better let me do that," Thompson said. "Nobody will think anything of seeing one of the employees putting a drunk to bed. Happens every night. The less attention we get, the better." He took the dead man's arm, draped it over his shoulder.

Liddell checked the hall, nodded.

The deputy walked out, the dead man's arm draped over his shoulder, Tommy supporting him at the waist. He crossed quickly to the rear exit, pushed his way through. Liddell followed.

In the truck they strapped the dead man onto the stretcher next to his partner. They covered him with another piece of discolored tarpaulin, locked the rear doors of the truck.

Liddell slid in behind the wheel, the deputy climbed onto the seat beside him.

"Better take the service entrance out," Tommy suggested. "Attract less attention." He reached over to the dashboard, snapped a switch. The turret on top of the truck started to blink red. "Nobody will stop us with that on. It's made more than one pickup here."

ELEVEN

The Las Palmas morgue was a one-story building set across from the General Hospital. Johnny Liddell wheeled the pickup truck down a ramp marked *Mortuary—Official Vehicles Only.*

At the foot of the ramp, there was a small loading platform with a wheeled stretcher in readiness. There was no sign of any employees.

Liddell jumped out of the truck, signaled for the deputy to wait. He walked to a large metal sliding door on the platform, tested it. It scraped open with an ear-jarring screech. Johnny waited for a moment, then entered the dim corridor that stretched beyond.

There were two glass doors on the left, both dark, and at the end of the hall there was a pair of double doors on which was stenciled *Mortuary—Employees Only.* He walked down to them, opened the doors a crack, satisfied himself the room beyond was empty.

He walked back to the truck.

"Looks like we have an all clear," he told Thompson. "Whoever made arrangements for our friends to find me new lodgings courtesy of the county saw to it they wouldn't be interrupted. Which makes it fine for us."

"The doc's a bottle baby. They probably got him

stoned out of his mind, put him to bed to keep him out of the way."

Liddell got into the truck, backed it up until its rear door was level with the loading platform. Thompson unlocked the door, helped Liddell transfer the dead man to the wheeled apparatus. Johnny pushed the body along the deserted corridor to the swinging doors.

Inside was a completely furnished receiving room where new arrivals were made ready for the vaults. Two freshly-scrubbed sandstone tables with individual drains stood under cone-shaped overhead lights. One wall was given up to a long glass-doored cabinet filled with surgical instruments. There was an overpowering smell of antiseptic spiced with another smell, heavy and unpleasant.

They wheeled the stretcher across the room to a heavy door set in the far wall. Liddell tugged it open. Beyond was a high-ceilinged, stone-floored, unheated room with double tiers of metal lockers. Each locker had its own number stenciled on it. Most of the lockers had a card on them with a name typewritten on it.

Liddell yanked at one of the drawers that had no name on it. He wrinkled his nose at the heavy, carbolic-laden air that rose from the drawer. It was empty.

"How do you like that for a lucky guy?" Liddell grunted. "Right at the height of the season and him with no reservations." He reached in, pulled out a crumpled canvas sheet.

Thompson grimaced at the stained sheet. "Don't look like they change the linen very often." He waited until Liddell had caught hold of the feet of the man on the stretcher, lifted the head. They slid the dead man into the drawer, covered him with the canvas and slammed the drawer shut with a clang that reverberated through the morgue.

"One good thing, we don't have to worry about disturbing the other guests. They're real sound sleepers," Liddell said.

"How about the other guy? What do we do with him?"

Liddell considered. "There's plenty of room in here for him. That way his friends won't have far to look in the morning."

Tommy frowned, looked at the tiers of drawers. "He'd smother in there, wouldn't he?"

"We can make up his bed for him out here. Just leave him on the stretcher for the night."

The frown dissolved into a broad grin. "I'd like to be here when he wakes up. I'll bet when they take those straps off him he takes off and never stops running."

Liddell chuckled. "You think he'll be running? There'll be a guy showing him what running really is. What do you figure the medical examiner's going to do when he walks in here in the morning with a hangover and the guy on the stretcher starts yelling?"

The deputy chuckled at the picture it evoked, watched while Liddell walked over, read the cards on some of the occupied drawers.

"Must be a big family named Doe in this town. There's sure a lot of Johns and Janes," Liddell noted.

The deputy grew serious. "Sheriff has a boy who don't know his own strength. Guy named Linehan. He gets his kicks out of working over vagrants and 'bos before he dumps them outside the city limits. Sometimes they don't last until the city limits, sometimes they pick them up a few miles out in the desert or along the road. Coroner John Does them, they get a week's free lodging here and then potter's field."

Liddell's eyes continued to skip along the cards on the drawers. He stopped suddenly. "Mike Klein," he read softly.

"What?"

The deputy crossed the room, stood aside while Liddell pulled open the drawer. It screeched raucously. Inside was a suggestively shaped bulge covered with the usual stained white canvas. Liddell caught hold of the canvas, pulled it back. Fat Mike's lifeless eyes stared upward. Liddell put the tips of his fingers at the side of the dead man's head, pushed. The skin was cold and clammy to the touch. He pointed to the hole near the top of the head.

"There's where the bullet entered. You can see the powder burns. Right?"

The deputy forced himself to look, nodded.

Liddell turned the dead face to the other side, showed him where the bullet had come through the jawbone. "There's the point of exit." He looked at the deputy bleakly. "That's all the proof you need that he was murdered." He stared down at Fat Mike. "They slipped on this one. The sheriff told me he was already embalmed."

"But how could we prove it?" His eyes skipped around the room, came to rest on the wheeled stretcher. "Unless we—"

"Steal the body?" Liddell contemplated the bulk of the dead man, shook his head. "He mightn't be such bad company in here. But once we get him out of here and that sun comes up in the morning—" He wrinkled his nose, shook his head. "There isn't that much ice in Las Palmas. Besides, where were you figuring on bedding him down? In my place? It would play hell with my social life."

"What then?"

Liddell frowned in concentration. "How would they do it if they wanted to keep the proof for officials' records?" he grumbled. He stared at the dead face for a moment, then snapped his fingers. "Pictures!"

He headed across the floor to the examining room, the deputy stared after him.

Inside, he walked to the cabinet of surgical instruments, walked from glass door to glass door until he found what he wanted. It was a long, thin, stainless steel rod. He tried the door, found it locked. With the piece of cellophane he carried in his wallet, he opened the door, picked out the rod. It was about fourteen inches long with the circumference of a narrow pencil.

He spent the next ten minutes vainly searching the room, finally admitted defeat, straightened up to face a curious Tommy Thompson standing in the doorway.

"What are you looking for?" the deputy wanted to know.

"A camera. You wouldn't happen to know where we could pick one up?"

"What kind of camera?"

"A Press or a 35 millimeter?"

Thompson shook his head. "I wouldn't know where to start looking. All I've got is a Polaroid that—"

"How soon could you get it here?"

The deputy scratched at his neck. "Ten, fifteen minutes."

Liddell consulted his watch. "It's a chance we've got to take." He caught the deputy by the arm. "Take the pickup truck. I'll make the other button comfortable." He ran inside, got the wheeled stretcher, led the way to the loading platform. Thompson helped him transfer the still unconscious gunman to the wheeled apparatus.

"You get the camera. I'll take care of him," Liddell told him.

The deputy nodded, jumped into the cab of the truck, roared it up the ramp.

Johnny Liddell sat on the side of an examining table,

smoking with short nervous puffs. He checked his watch for the fourth time, realized it was less than three minutes since the last time he looked at it. It was almost twenty minutes since Thompson had left for his camera. He could only hope that the two gunmen had made sure of the medical examiner for the whole night. It seemed probable since they had no way of knowing how late Liddell would be returning to his room.

He crushed his cigarette out on the side of the table, tossed the butt at a white enameled refuse pail. Nobody had to tell him how close he'd come to being one of the John Does who were enjoying the temporary facilities of the inside room before taking the one-way ride to Las Palmas's potter's field.

He stiffened, listened. The sound of the truck coming down the ramp was unmistakable. Liddell vaulted off the table, stepped behind the swinging door. He rested his hand on the butt of the .45. It had a satisfyingly reassuring feeling.

The doors burst open, Thompson ran in. "Sorry to take so long, Liddell. I had to tear the place apart to find it. Haven't used it much since I got out here. I just hope the film is still good." He walked over to the examining table, broke open the camera. He took what was left of an old roll out, inserted a new roll, straightened up. "We'll never be in a better position to find out."

Liddell led the way into the refrigerated room, tugged open the drawer containing Fat Mike. Grimacing, he caught the dead man under the neck, pulled him to a sitting position, closed the drawer until it supported Mike's back. He reached up, pulled on a high-powered light in an enamel reflector.

"Let's get a close shot of the place of entry," Liddell told the deputy.

Tommy adjusted the flash on the camera, aimed it

close to the dead man's head, clicked the shutter. He straightened up, looked over to where the other gunman lay, strapped to the stretcher. "Sleeping Beauty still out?"

Liddell grinned bleakly. "He's waiting for his Fairy Prince to kiss him." He looked back to the deputy. "That only takes a minute. Right? Shouldn't it be done by now?"

The deputy consulted his watch, nodded. "In a few seconds." He watched the second hand on his watch crawl around to the twenty, then fumbled with the catch on the back of the camera. He brought out a clear close-up of Fat Mike's head, handed it to Liddell.

"Science is sure wonderful," Liddell conceded. "He takes a beautiful picture. The film's okay, so let's get a couple of shots of the direction of the bullet, then a couple of insurance shots on the point of entry."

"How do we get the angle shot?"

"You ever work homicide in New York?"

The deputy shook his head. "Never got into plainclothes even."

Liddell picked up the steel rod. "Homicide always establishes the angle of the wound in pictures by putting a pencil or anything like that in the wound." He fumbled with the rod for a moment, straightened up. One end of the rod protruded from the point of entry. The other from the point of exit of the bullet. "Get me a couple of good pictures of that, and we'll have no trouble at all proving Fat Mike was murdered." He watched while Tommy shot another picture, waited until he removed it from the back of the camera, nodded. "Just for insurance, let's get a couple more. Then some close ones of the powder burns on top."

Tommy Thompson nodded, swallowed hard. In the bright light, his complexion seemed to have taken on a greenish tinge, his mouth was circled by a white ring. He put the camera into position, snapped another shot.

Fat Mike sat, propped up in the drawer, staring at the far wall with eyes that would never see again. But they were the only eyes that were in the proper position to see the man on the stretcher open his eyes, stare around and fix on the two men standing at the open drawer. His eyes saw and understood. Cautiously, he tested the straps that bound him to the stretcher. A thin sheen of perspiration glistened on his face as he struggled. Then, abruptly, he stopped struggling, continued to watch the picture-taking from between slitted lids.

TWELVE

Sheriff Tom Regan sat behind his desk the next morning, stared malevolently at the two men who stood facing him.

Doc Sam Green was a thin, balding man in his late fifties, with a perpetually damp nose and runny eyes. He was extremely nervous, kept clearing his throat with short, barking coughs. His hand shook noticeably as he raised it to the discolored tip of his nose.

"You were supposed to have Fat Mike all fixed up by yesterday afternoon. Why wasn't he?" Regan growled.

The medical examiner dry-washed bloodless hands, twisted his mouth into what was obviously an unfamiliar smile. "I—I got tied up. Sheriff," he quavered. "I—I didn't get around to it."

"Tied up doing what? Trying to drink the town dry?" Regan leaned forward, poked a stubby finger in the direction of the thin man. "You know what you did? You put your neck on the line. That shamus has pictures proving Mike Klein didn't commit suicide. And you signed the death certificate."

Doc Green barked loudly, made a futile attempt to clear his throat. "That's what you wanted me to certify, Sheriff. You told me yourself—"

98

Regan leaned back, shook his head. "I don't know what you're talking about." He studied the doctor's face, tried to gauge the degree of apprehension. "All I do know is that if the state police get their hands on those pictures, you may have some questions to answer. And you got nobody to thank but yourself. If you fixed him up like you were told, this couldn't have happened."

Green's hand twisting became more frenzied. "How could I know anybody would break into the morgue?" He shook his head bewilderedly. "You were the one who asked me to give the attendant the night off."

The sheriff agreed. "Only because I expected you to stand in for him. But no. You had to get hold of a bottle and get blind."

The medical examiner licked at his lips. "I was fixing to take care of Mike today. I didn't figure on—"

"You didn't figure, period." The white-haired man scowled at Doc Green. "Make sure you don't pull any other boners." He rolled his eyes over to the calendar on the wall. "Today's Thursday. That's shipping day for the John Does. Right?"

The medical examiner cleared his throat, nodded his head. "That's another thing, Sheriff. This morning I got one more than I have on my manifest." He barked nervously, his Adam's apple bobbing. "I got no papers and no records on him—"

"Ship him out today with the other floaters."

"But my records—"

The sheriff leaned forward. "That's your problem. You take a stiff in and forget to book him, don't blame me. If you're smart, you'll get rid of him and have that morgue in good shape in case that shamus does manage to reach the state police. You follow me?"

Green licked at his lips. "I—I think so."

"I hope you do. For your sake." He squinted at him.

"You'd better be getting back to the morgue. Sounds like you have a busy day ahead of you."

The medical examiner looked from the man at his side to the sheriff, nodded. "I guess I have." He turned, scampered from the room.

When the door slammed behind the medical examiner, the sheriff turned his eyes on the other man. He stared at him with no sign of enthusiasm. "You sure bolloxed things up real good, Bauer," he snarled. "All you got to do is deliver this shamus to the morgue so we can John Doe him with the shipment today. So what do you do? You end up in the morgue yourself and your partner takes the ride."

The thin man glared at him sullenly. "If it wasn't for me, you wouldn't know about those pictures."

The sheriff snorted. "If it wasn't for you, there wouldn't be any pictures. Your partner doesn't walk away from Liddell and you give him the what-with to get rid of the body. We can't even tag him for the kill."

"Look, Regan, I don't like it either. I damn near froze to death in that morgue all night. I can't breathe for the stink. And then when that bottlehead coroner of yours come in, he takes one look at me and runs out screaming. Then I got to explain to the broad that works for him it's a practical joke. Some guys think it's a great gag to lock me up in there overnight."

Regan got up from his desk, walked to the window, stared out for a moment. Then he walked back to his desk. "We've got to get those pictures."

"How?"

The sheriff dropped into his desk chair. "That story you told the girl in doc's office. She buy it?"

Bauer shrugged. "I didn't wait to find out. All I wanted was to get out from under that sheet and get a

100

few belts into me." His hand shook slightly as he raised it, flattened the hair over his ear with the heel of his palm. "You don't know what it's like being strapped to one of those death carts, laying in a vault all night unless you've tried it."

"All right, all right. So it was rugged. Your buddy didn't enjoy it either. And he didn't get to leave." Regan picked up a pencil from his desk top, doodled on a pad. "How about the girl? You think she bought your story?"

Bauer shrugged again. "She had to know I didn't strap myself on."

The sheriff nodded thoughtfully. "Okay. She's going to make a complaint, you're going to finger Liddell as the practical joker. We're going to run him in for disorderly conduct, defacing civic property, anything we can think of." He tossed the pencil back on the desk, leaned back. "From there on, it's Ted Linehan's job to persuade the shamus that he's not welcome around here."

"But what about my buddy? If Liddell tells what really happened—"

"By then your buddy will be out in potter's field with five or six other boxes on top of him to keep him down. Leave that to Doc Green. He's got too much to lose to goof on this one."

Bauer considered it, liked it. "And you take the pictures away from Liddell and all he's left with is a practical joke that backfired." He thought it over some more, nodded. "I buy it."

"Okay." Regan reached for the phone, dialed a number. "Let me talk to the medical examiner," he told the girl on the other end. "This is Sheriff Regan."

There was a short pause, then the sound of the medical examiner's barking cough came through. "Yes, Sheriff?" His voice quavered.

"Bauer here was telling me about the outrage that was committed at the morgue last night. He's willing to identify the man responsible."

"G—Good."

Regan raked at his thick white hair with clenched fingers. "The girl in your office—what's her name?"

"Myra. Myra Downey."

Regan nodded. "She saw the effect the outrage had on you, got a bad scare herself. Is that right?"

"Yes."

"The disturbance was upsetting enough to make you forget the actual count of John Does, isn't that right?"

The voice on the other end quavered. "I—that is, Sheriff—"

Regan ignored the interruption. "Well, we don't stand for that kind of disregard for law and order. I want you to have your Miss Downey file a complaint. Bauer here will identify the man responsible. We'll see to it that nothing like this happens again."

"If—you say so, Sheriff."

"How about that extra John Doe—"

The bark came over the wire. "I—I found the papers on him, Sheriff. He—he's on the list to go out this morning."

Regan looked over to where Bauer stood, smiled. "Good. I want you to make sure your girl gets right on this. As soon as she's made the complaint, my office will act."

"I'll get right at it."

The sheriff dropped the receiver back on its hook, peered at the man across the desk. "Let's see if we can do it right, this time." He punched a button on the base of his phone, lifted the receiver to his ear. "Tell Linehan I want to see him."

The man on the other side of the desk dropped into a chair, dug a pack of cigarettes out of his pocket. He lit one, leaned back. He was still having trouble controlling the shaking of his hand.

Bauer was halfway through with his cigarette when the door opened and Ted Linehan walked in. He was big, heavy-shouldered, wore the tag "cop" all over him. Even his shoes looked as if they should be wearing a badge. His blue suit was rumpled, a stained fedora was pushed to the back of his head. He was picking his teeth as he walked in. He looked at Bauer incuriously, rolled his beady eyes to the man behind the desk.

"You wanted to see me, Sheriff?"

"You sure weren't in any hurry to find out," Regan growled.

"You didn't say nothing about being in a hurry." He poked at a molar with a black-rimmed thumbnail. "What's up?"

"There's a private detective in town. Name's Liddell. He's registered at Fat Mike's place—" He looked to Bauer inquiringly.

"Bungalow 8, 1D."

"Liddell went on a tear last night, broke up some city property, busted into the morgue and as a gag left Bauer here tied to a stretcher." He looked to Bauer. "That right?"

The man in the chair nodded.

Regan turned back to the man in the rumpled suit. "Medical examiner's office is willing to press malicious mischief charges, Bauer here is ready to put the finger on Liddell. Bring him in."

Linehan snuffled noisily through a broken nose, licked at his lips. "If he puts up any kind of a fight?"

"You've handled that kind before."

103

Linehan shrugged hulking shoulders. "Just asking."

Regan nodded, checked his watch. "Give it an hour or two before you pick him up. We want everything nice and legal. By then Doc Green's office will have the complaint on the JP's blotter."

The plainclothesman nodded. He waited for further instructions, when none were forthcoming he turned and shuffled toward the door. As soon as Linehan had closed the door behind him, the sheriff turned to Bauer. "When Linehan picks him up, I want you to go through Liddell's bungalow with a fine-tooth comb. We've got to get those pictures back."

The man in the chair nodded. "We'll get them."

The sheriff fixed him with a jaundiced eye. "We'd better!"

Johnny Liddell stood with Lee Loomis at the 21 table, watched while the redhead scratched her card for the dealer to hit her sixteen again. The next card was a five of hearts. She purred contentedly, nodded that she was finished. The dealer turned to the next player, laid an eight on her fourteen. The woman groaned, turned up her case card. The dealer flipped his hidden card over, revealed it to be the ace of hearts. With no change of expression, he lifted the top card off the deck, laid it next to the ace. It was the queen of spades.

"Twenty-one," he grunted.

The redhead scowled at him, watched him lift the small pile of silver dollars from in front of her, add it to those in his rack. She started to say something, stopped as she saw the heavy-shouldered man step behind Liddell.

"Your name Liddell?" the newcomer wanted to know.

Liddell started to turn toward the man, winced at the feel of the gun snout in his back.

104

"When you turn, make it real slow," the big man told him.

Liddell turned around, studied the broken nose, the thick cruel lips and the beady eyes of Linehan. He dropped his eyes to the snub-nosed .38 in the plain-clothesman's hand. "What is this?"

"Your name Liddell?" Linehan repeated.

"Yeah."

A coarse tongue licked at the thick lips. "You're under arrest." The beady eyes swept the small group around the table. "This doesn't concern any of you. This man is wanted for questioning on a number of charges. Don't get in my way." He scowled as he recognized the uniform of a special deputy working his way over to the table.

Tommy Thompson walked up, looked inquiringly at the dealer. "What goes on?" His hand rested on the butt of the .45 in his holster.

"Police business," Linehan grunted. "This man's my prisoner."

Thompson scowled at him, looked toward the ceiling. "Police business or not, Mac. Don't ever show a rod in this place. There are three guys up there with shotguns on you." He looked at Liddell, caught the barely perceptible signal to stay out of it. "I suppose you got paper to prove this man's wanted?"

Linehan dug into his jacket pocket, pulled out a warrant, tossed it to the deputy.

Tommy read it, nodded. "Okay. You won't need the rod. I'll help you get him out to the car. We wouldn't like any disturbance in here." He signaled to the men behind the peephole in the ceiling. "Like I said, if you want to stay in one piece don't ever flash iron in this place again." He nodded to the dealer. "Okay, Eddie, go on with your game. I'll take it from here." He nodded for Liddell and the plainclothesman to follow him.

At the entrance, he stopped. "I'll keep him here while you get your car. By the way, what's he wanted for?"

Linehan grunted, shrugged. "Half a dozen things. Malicious mischief, kidnaping, breaking and entering." He favored Liddell with a sour look. "This was a real busy boy last night." He stepped out, looked to the rear of the porte-cochere. "My car's right back here. I won't be a minute."

As soon as Linehan was out of earshot, Thompson turned to Liddell. "You want to lay one on me and make a run for it?" he asked in a low voice.

Liddell shook his head.

"These are real rough boys, Liddell. Once they get you in that basement room, they play for keeps."

"I'm not exactly a daisy chain myself. It will give me a chance to find out just how deeply the sheriff is mixed up in whatever's going on around here." He watched for the plainclothesman's return. "And they won't do anything final with me until they know just how much I do know."

"How about the pictures? They may know about them—"

"They'll search my room, if they do."

"And the pictures?"

Liddell saw Linehan step into a black car at the far end. "I sent one set addressed to myself at General Delivery, one set addressed to you. If they get too rough, I can always deliver the set that's in my name."

The black car skidded to a stop in front of the entrance. Thompson nudged Liddell's arm, led him to the open back door where Linehan sat in the far corner, his .38 cradled in the crook of his elbow. Liddell slid into the back seat opposite him.

"Good luck," Thompson said.

106

Linehan grinned, licked at his lips. "He's sure going to need it," he grunted. "And don't worry about him giving you any more trouble. We'll see to it that he gets out of town."

THIRTEEN

Sheriff Tom Regan was hunched over a game of solitaire when Ted Linehan pushed open the door to his office, sent Liddell reeling in. The sheriff pursed his lips, shook his head at the cards.

"Some days it don't even pay to get out of bed."

He opened his top drawer, scooped the cards into it, looked up at Liddell. "So you decided not to take my advice, huh, Liddell?" he asked sadly. "Could have saved us all a lot of trouble. Mine's ending, but I'm afraid yours is just beginning."

Liddell considered it. "Mind telling me what this is all about?"

The sheriff looked hurt. "You're not going to treat me like some hick sheriff, I hope." He reached into his basket, brought out a sheet of paper. His eyes skipped over it, rolled up to Liddell. "The medical examiner's office is charging you with malicious mischief, destruction of county property, breaking and entering." He sucked at his front teeth, let it sink in. "A visitor to town named Larry Bauer is charging you with atrocious assault, kidnaping and a couple of other things." He shook his head.

"I could toss you in the pokey and throw away the key for half of what you did."

"But?"

Regan shrugged. "I might give you a break. Sort of professional courtesy, you might say." He studied Liddell's expression. "But I'm not quashing these complaints. Just sort of letting them pend. The next time I saw you in town I'd have to enforce them."

"That's mighty generous of you, Sheriff," Liddell said. "But suppose I decided not to take you up on your kind offer?"

Regan leaned back, pursed his lips, looked thoughtful. "That could be a mighty unfortunate decision. For you." He narrowed his eyes, peered at Liddell. "What are you really snooping around for, shamus? You got your money from Fat Mike. Now what are you after? A merit badge?"

"For one thing, I want the man who killed Fat Mike."

Regan's eyes swept from Liddell to Linehan and back. He shook his head. "We're not going that route again, are we? Mike Klein was sick, so he committed suicide."

"Not in my book. And I intend to prove it."

"What's getting into this town? Everybody got a suicide complex?" Regan complained. "We know something about what went on in the vault last night. You don't think you can walk away with those pictures?"

"Now we're getting down to cases," Liddell said.

The white-haired man nodded his head. "It's all among friends. It won't be going out of this room." He studied Liddell's face. "We're going to get those pictures Liddell, one way or another. You can make it easy on yourself by handing them over. Or"—he looked significantly at Linehan—"our friend here will have the pleasure of taking them off you."

Liddell scowled. "It's been tried."

"Why waste time, Sheriff? There's nothing I like better than taking the starch out of these tough guys. When I'm done with them they're like Jello—nice and shaky," Linehan put in. "Let me work him over. He'll be begging to tell you everything he knows."

The sheriff raised his eyebrows at Liddell, was interrupted by the ringing of the phone. He lifted the receiver to his ear, scowled, fixed his eyes on Liddell.

"You're sure?"

He listened to the explanation from the other end, said, "Okay, we'll handle it from here." He dropped the receiver on its hook, glared at Liddell. "The pictures aren't in your bungalow."

"I could have saved you the trouble."

"He's all yours, Linehan. I want those pictures. I don't care what you have to do to get them."

The big man chuckled deep in his chest. "Leave him to me, Sheriff."

Liddell backed away until he felt the wall at his back.

"You're not being smart, Liddell. Linehan's an officer of the law. Fight back and we add a resisting arrest charge to the rest."

"Might as well try for the jackpot." Liddell kept his eyes on the big man, watched as he hunched his head between his shoulders, started shuffling toward him.

"Resist arrest and Linehan could plug you right where you stand," the sheriff tried to divert Liddell's attention.

Suddenly, the strong-arm cop made his move. He shot a right at Liddell's head. Johnny swayed out of its path, brought up a left that Linehan fielded with his midsection. The air whooshed out of his lungs like a punctured balloon.

The plainclothesman stepped back for a moment, re-

110

covered. He growled like a stung bear, bored in. He caught Liddell on the side of his head with a hamlike fist that started lights flashing and bells ringing in Liddell's head. Johnny back-pedaled, tried to get out of the way of the punishing right hand, but it landed again and Liddell had the sensation of the floor tilting, coming up and hitting him in the face.

The sheriff walked around the desk, turned Liddell over on his back with the toe of his shoe. He looked up to where Linehan stood, his breath snuffling noisily through his smashed nose.

"See if he has those pictures on him."

The plainclothesman nodded, knelt alongside Liddell, emptied his pockets into a little pile alongside him. He pocketed the small roll of bills he took from Johnny's pants pocket, brought the rest of his belongings to the sheriff's desk. The sheriff went through Liddell's wallet, flipped through the pages of a small memo book he carried, examined his keys and cards hoping to find some evidence that he had checked the photographs.

Finally Regan leaned back, shook his head. "No sign of them." He scowled thoughtfully. "He might have given them to somebody to hold. Bauer said there was a guy working with him last night. A guy in a deputy's uniform."

"He make the deputy?"

The white-haired man shook his head. "His back was turned." He looked down at Liddell. "Maybe you could get the shamus to confide in you. You think?"

Linehan grinned wolfishly. "When we're done with him he's going to sound like he's been mainlining with a phonograph needle." He walked over to the desk, picked up the phone, pressed the button on its base. "This is Ted Linehan. I'm in the sheriff's office. Tell Pete Breck

I want him in here right away." He dropped the receiver on its hook. "It's like we're real persuasive, Sheriff. These tough guys, they're a pleasure to break. When they crack, they go all the way."

Regan nodded. "Get the pictures first. Then have all the fun you want."

There was a knock on the door, the door opened and a man who could have been Ted Linehan's twin walked in. His eyes hopscotched from Linehan to the sheriff to the floor where Johnny Liddell was beginning to groan his way back to consciousness.

"Sheriff wants us to play Twenty Questions with this shamus. I thought you might like to get in on the fun, Pete. I can use a hand getting him down to the basement."

Pete Breck nodded. They both walked over to where Liddell lay, caught him under the arms, pulled him to his feet and half carried, half dragged him out of the office.

The basement of the County Courthouse had no windows. Its walls were plain cinder block painted a dun color. The door was thick, fitted closely, making the room almost soundproof.

Breck pushed the door open, waited until Linehan had dragged Liddell in, then closed the door. Linehan dumped Liddell on a hard wooden chair, shucked off his jacket and tossed it across a table near the wall. He stared at Liddell who sat in the chair with his head rolling uncontrollably from side to side. He seemed to lack the power to lift it.

Pete Breck walked over, joined his partner. "So this is one of those tough New York private eyes?" He reached over, caught a handful of Liddell's hair, pulled his head back. Liddell seemed to be having trouble focusing his eyes. "This one hasn't even got as much fight in him as

112

that 'bo we picked up at the railroad station." He grinned appreciatively. "He sure put up a fight, didn't he? Too bad that skull of his cracked so easy. Guy like that around for a week or so could keep a man in real good condition."

Linehan studied Liddell's face. "You going to make it easy on yourself, shamus? Where's the pictures?"

Liddell's eyes continued to roll. A thin stream of saliva glistened from the corner of his mouth. Breck dropped his head disgustedly. "He don't even know his own name."

Linehan grabbed Liddell by the tie, pulled him to his feet. He chopped at the side of Liddell's neck, knocked him to his knees. He kicked at his face, Liddell rolled with the kick, took it on the shoulder, fell back on the floor.

The plainclothesman spat down at him, stood over him, hands on hips, feet astraddle. "He'll talk," he grunted. "Soon's we soften him up a bit." He raised his foot to stamp Liddell, was momentarily off balance.

Liddell put everything he had into a sudden upward thrust of his heels. Linehan's face turned an ugly purple, his eyes popped as Johnny's heels sank into his groin. He sank to his knees, gargled noisily for breath, tumbled forward, hit the stone floor face first with an ugly plop.

Pete Breck stood stunned by the sudden turn of events. Before he could swing into action, Liddell was on his feet. The cop tugged a leather-covered sap from his pocket, tried to swing it. Liddell caught him a paralyzing chop above the wrist, the blackjack fell to the floor.

Liddell reached up, wiped the beaded perspiration from his upper lip with the side of his hand, started for Breck flat-footedly. He missed a hard left, took a right jab that sent him staggering back on his heels. He shook

113

his head, recovered in time to see Breck going for his holster. Before the plainclothesman's gun could clear leather, Liddell was all over him. He caught the gun hand in a viselike grip, bent it back behind the man.

Breck struggled, tried to bring his knee up, lost leverage when Liddell stuck his head under the plainclothesman's chin, pushing it upward and backward. Perspiration broke out in gleaming beads all over Breck's face as slowly, inexorably Liddell bent him back over his own arm. The plainclothesman screamed out in pain, the gun fell from his damp fingers, hit the floor. Liddell sent it spinning to the corner of the room with a kick.

Liddell released his hammerlock on Breck, let him fall to the floor. The only sound in the room was the heavy breathing of the two men and the snuffling, whimpering of the semiconscious Linehan on the floor.

Liddell started for the gun at the other end of the room, Breck pulled himself to his feet, stood between Johnny and the .38. As Liddell started to circle him, Breck darted forward, sank his left into Johnny's midsection, took a smashing right to the eye in return. He took the punch well, kept boring in relentlessly. Liddell back-pedaled, made the big man come to him.

Suddenly Liddell stopped his backward movement, planted his feet, lashed out with both hands. The maneuver caught Breck off balance. He took a straight right to the jaw, an uppercut to the throat that made him gag. Liddell continued to throw both hands, sank his left to the cuff in the other's middle. Breck retched, gasped open-mouthed for air.

Liddell moved in. He crossed his right to the other man's unprotected jaw. The plainclothesman's eyes turned glassy; he made a feeble effort to lash out at Liddell but seemed to have lost all co-ordination. Liddell chopped at the base of Breck's neck, the big man's knees folded under him. He hit the floor with a thud, lay there face down, didn't move.

Liddell stood over him for a moment, swaying. Then, he walked over to a sink in the corner, stuck his head under the cold tap and washed away the fuzziness. He picked up the gun from against the wall, walked over to where Linehan lay, still semiconscious. He turned him over, tugged the .38 from his holster.

He was swabbing at his damp face and hair with a towel when the door to the basement screeched open. Liddell crouched, covered the door with the two guns.

Sheriff Regan appeared in the doorway. He stopped stock-still, his eyes popping. He looked from Liddell to the two men on the floor and back. His lips moved but no sound came out.

"Come in and join the party, Sheriff," Liddell told him.

The sheriff eyed the two guns, stepped in with alacrity. Behind him stood Martin Sommers. He took the situation in with a glance.

"Put up the guns, Liddell," the tanned man told him. He turned to Regan. "You're going to have a lot of explaining to do, Regan."

"I told you, Mr. Sommers. We have a complaint on him for kidnaping and half a dozen other things."

"Try holding him on them, and you'll have the damnedest false arrest suit you ever had thrown at you. You knew Liddell was working for us."

Regan shrugged sulkily. "I got my job to do, Mr. Sommers. I get a complaint handed to me, I got to make the arrest."

Sommers turned back to Liddell. "What's been going on down here?"

Liddell shrugged. "The sheriff and his boys were betting I'd be begging them to take some pictures off my hands. They lost."

Regan considered it, shook his head. "I told you it was a mistake to keep considering me a hick sheriff, shamus. Even way out here we see those private eye shows where the hero is so smart he mails things to himself General Delivery." He walked over, filled a metal pail with water, dumped it over Linehan, was rewarded by a gasp. He looked over at Liddell. "You might want to have a look at Fat Mike Klein before he's shipped back home. They did a real great job on' him." The corners of the sheriff's lips tilted upward. "You couldn't even tell he was shot— let alone where."

Sommers's eyes hopped from the sheriff to Liddell and back. "What's this all about?"

Liddell grinned bleakly. "It looks like the sheriff and I have just played a game of Mexican stand-off," he said. He eyed Sommers curiously. "How'd you happen to drop by to do the Marines bit?"

"Fat Mike's girl—the redhead—"

"Lee Loomis?"

The tanned man nodded. "She called, told me the law had dragged you out of the Music Hall. Since you're still technically working for us, I came right over to see what I could do." He swiveled his eyes to the sheriff. "It took a while for the sheriff to remember which way you'd gone." He eyed the white-haired man. "Any reason why he can't walk out with me?"

The sheriff dropped his eyes to Linehan who was sputtering his way back to consciousness, jackknifed on the floor. "I would like to see Ted get a chance to even things," he conceded. "But there's always another time."

Liddell skidded the two guns across the room, out of

116

reach. "I'll keep a place on my dance card for him." He turned, limped after Martin Sommers. Behind him, he could hear the sheriff expressing a highly censorable, and at best debatable, opinion of his two men, their personal habits, their legitimacy and the possible canine element in their immediate families.

FOURTEEN

Martin Sommers settled back against the cushions in the rear seat of the Cadillac, waited until Johnny Liddell had sunk down beside him. As soon as the door was closed, the driver eased the car into gear, slid away from the curb outside the County Courthouse.

Liddell dug into his pocket, brought up a pack of cigarettes. He held it out to the tanned man, drew a shake of the head.

"Now, suppose you tell me what it was really about?"

Liddell stuck a cigarette in the corner of his mouth, touched a match to it. He filled his lungs with smoke, blew it at the ceiling of the car. "The sheriff's boys and I were trying to impress each other with how tough we were. They weren't."

Sommers snorted impatiently. "What was this bit about pictures?"

Liddell grimaced. "I got into the morgue last night. Fat Mike's body was there. I took some pictures that would prove he had been murdered." He shrugged. "I tried to protect them by mailing them to myself. But I guess I downgraded the sheriff too much. When he

118

didn't find them at my place or on me, he tried the post office."

"Why are you so determined to prove Mike was murdered? I told you we'd prefer to leave things as they are."

Liddell blew out a stream of smoke, watching it curl toward the air conditioning vents. "Because Mike hired me. He wasn't much good and his being hit is no great loss to the community. But he was my client and I don't like people who knock off my clients."

"I'm your client, too. So are Lewine, Morrow and Rossi," Sommers reminded him.

Liddell grinned at him. "So I'll feel the same way about anybody who tries for you."

"You won't have to. We're not about to make the same mistake twice. We heard from the shake artist again. We make the payoff tonight." He turned, stared out the window. "I told him you were going to handle it for us. He stood still for it."

"When and where?"

Sommers looked back at him, frowned slightly. "I don't know. You're to be at a ringside table at Fat Mike's place for the first show. He'll contact you there." The frown deepened. "But you're beginning to worry me, Liddell. You apparently aren't very good at following instructions."

Liddell met his gaze levelly. "I don't know about that. So far, the only instructions I've had were to find the guy who killed Larry Adams. Since it figures that the same guy killed Fat Mike, I've been trying to get a line on him. That's what I was hired for. Remember?"

Sommers nodded, the worried frown still on his face. "You were also told to let it lay. Instead, you break into the morgue and pull a lot of theatrics that do nothing but cause trouble." He tilted his head back, studied the ceiling. "You know a guy named Carl Jensen?"

119

"Yeah. I met him at Benny Lewine's place last night."

The eyes rolled down from the ceiling, fixed on Liddell's face. "That the only time you met him?"

Liddell shook his head. "I dropped by to take a look at his set-up downtown. Penny ante stuff. But he won't be there forever."

"He's a real ambitious guy. A real redhot." Sommers pursed his lips. "If he keeps pushing Benny, he's liable to get cooled off. Real quick."

Liddell feigned polite surprise. "Pushing Benny?"

"He's been eyeing Benny's operation for a long time. This morning he dropped by, had a talk with Benny. Seems he thinks Benny could use a new casino boss."

"Namely him?"

Sommers nodded. "He mentioned to Benny that he has some connections in New York. You knew both Benny and Fat Mike are from New York?"

Liddell nodded.

"Well, it seems that Jensen figures some of Mike's old buddies in New York would be interested to know he was murdered." He peered at Liddell, wrinkles alongside his eyes cutting white trenches in the tan. "Those same contacts might start asking a lot of questions, such as why didn't Benny handle things for Mike."

"And then the whole story of the shake would come out and the boys up north would figure you fellows down here have lost control."

"Something like that."

Liddell considered it. "How was Jensen figuring to prove Mike was murdered?"

"Maybe he was counting on you doing it for him. Maybe you even agreed to handle the contract for him?"

Liddell shook his head. "I only work for one guy at a time."

"Then what made you drop by to see him?"

"I had him pegged as a possible for the shake artist. He fits the role real good. Young, ambitious and on the make. A million could put a guy like that in real solid."

Sommers looked thoughtful. "It could be somebody like that," he conceded. "So what did you stand to gain by telling him Mike and Larry had been murdered?"

"I wanted to jolt him into making a move. That's when they make their big mistakes. When they're stampeded into moving."

"You really think he could be the shake artist?"

Liddell shrugged. "Maybe. Maybe not. He was really shaken up when I told him they had been hit in the head. The shake artist wouldn't be." He took a last drag on the cigarette, crushed it out in the arm-rest ash tray. "Jensen is muscle. Even between his ears. He only knows one thing—get your foot in the door, then muscle the rest of the way in. The shake artist has some imagination."

Sommers agreed. "You could be right." He looked out the window. "We're at your place. I'll drop you off here." He leaned forward, rapped on the glass panel that separated the driver from the back seat. The driver nodded.

"About tonight," Liddell put in. "You still want me to handle it?"

Sommers leaned back, worried his lower lip with his thumb and forefinger. "I told him it would be you. But that was before I heard how busy you've been since you hit town." He frowned his annoyance. "He might get the idea we were pulling something if we were to change our plans. Can we count on you to follow instructions and not try to grandstand?"

"If you'd rather I didn't—"

Sommers sighed. "It's not that. We just don't want you to pull anything. It's our dough and we're willing to pay off. We don't want to buy any more grief."

The car pulled onto the porte-cochere, eased to a stop.

Liddell nodded. "Like you say, it's your dough. Where do I get it?"

"We're raising it now," Sommers answered. "And don't think it's easy. You'll be at the first show at the Music Hall tonight. Right?"

Liddell nodded.

"I'll have one of the boys leave it in the checkroom. He'll slip you the check."

"And I'll be hearing from the shake artist. Right?"

"I hope so. The sooner this is over and done with, the better we'll like it. Just play it straight. Don't let anything go wrong."

Liddell nodded. He reached over, pushed open the door. "By the way, I haven't thanked you for coming to the rescue."

Sommers smiled bleakly. "Looked to me like you were doing just fine without any help from anybody."

Liddell grinned. "From the look on the sheriff's face, it came as a bit of a surprise to him."

"I can imagine." Sommers told him dryly. He watched while Liddell stepped out of the car. "But tonight. No surprises."

Liddell nodded. He slammed the door, the car eased into motion. He stood on the porte-cochere until the big Cadillac had reached the highway, blended into the stream of traffic.

Liddell walked into the casino, looked around. There was no sign of the redhead. Toward the rear of the room, Tommy Thompson was standing, arms folded across his chest, eyes hopscotching around the room. They stopped when he saw Liddell, gave no sign of recognition. Liddell thought of walking over to him, remembered the peephole check kept on the floor from the ceiling gallery. Instead, he worked his way toward the pool exit. Outside, he headed across toward Bungalow 8.

He had expected some signs of a search in his room but he wasn't prepared for the extent of the damage. Drawers had been pulled open, their contents spilled on the floor. The bedding had been ripped off, mattresses dumped. The doors to the lavatory and the closet were ajar, gave evidence that the search had been continued in there. His bags and the rest of the contents of the closet had been searched and thrown aside.

Liddell swore under his breath, crossed to the closet. His shoulder harness was still hanging from a hook, but the .45 was gone. Frantically, he pawed through the mess on the floor hoping the searcher had been content to remove the magazine and toss the gun aside. After a ten-minute search, he gave it up. He was standing in the middle of the room, hands on hips, feet apart when a knock came at the door. He opened it a crack. The deputy was standing in the hallway.

Liddell opened the door. Thompson walked in. He looked around, whistled noiselessly. "Mice?"

"Rats." Liddell slammed the door.

"Lose anything important?"

"My .45. Know where I can lay my hands on a spare?"

Thompson nodded. "I'll dig one up for you. A snub-nosed .38 do?"

"Right now even a beanshooter would be an improvement."

The deputy eyed him curiously. "Looks like Sommers got to the sheriff's office in time. You're not marked at all."

123

"You ought to see the other guys."

"Guys?"

Liddell nodded. "Your buddy Linehan and another guy named Pete—"

"Breck. The other strong-arm man in the sheriff's office."

"They took me to the basement for a singing lesson. But Linehan's doing the singing. His voice changed this afternoon. And that Breck type will be eating through a straw for a while to come."

"This I would love to have seen."

"How about Lee? She all right?"

The deputy nodded. "They're running through the routines for the opening night. I'll get word back to her that you're okay. Anything else I can do?"

Liddell shook his head. "You haven't been to the post office?"

"I haven't had time. But when I go off I can—"

"Don't. The pictures are safer there. Regan got mine."

"I thought you said you didn't—"

"He didn't get them from me. Your sheriff is no fool. When he didn't find them here or on me, he tried the post office. He's been around awhile."

The deputy looked impressed. "I wouldn't have figured him for that smart an operator." He glanced at his watch. "I'd better get back on the floor. Whitey might notice I'm gone."

"How about this guy Whitey?"

Thompson shrugged. "No worse than the rest of them."

"Smart?"

The deputy considered. "He can take care of himself in the clinches. He's been doing a pretty good job of taking over for Mike. Things are running pretty smooth topside."

"Mike got hit by somebody he knew and trusted. Think it could have been Whitey?"

"Could be. I don't think it would keep Whitey awake nights if he knocked off his mother. But why?"

Liddell shrugged. "You just said yourself he's running things real smooth. Chances are the boys up north won't rock the boat, they'll let him keep running."

The deputy hesitated for a minute, then shrugged. "I guess it's no secret any more. Whitey wouldn't have to knock Mike off to get the casino. Mike was getting ready to move on."

Liddell frowned. "Move on?"

"Yeah. Since tourists started staying away from the Havana casinos in droves, things have been getting real hot in Mexico. Mike was getting ready to open up in Tia Juana. Make a play for the big Hollywood trade."

"You sure?"

"I should be. He was taking me with him. I was going to be floor boss in the casino. Whitey was staying here to run the Music Hall."

"Whitey know about the Tia Juana set-up?"

The deputy shook his head. "All Whitey knew was that Fat Mike was getting set to step out and had fixed it with the boys for Whitey to stand in for him. That's all Whitey was interested in."

"Who else knew about it?"

Thompson shrugged. "I don't know. Mike told me, but he made me promise to keep it under my hat until they were ready to move."

"They?"

"Larry Adams was in it with him. It was too big an

125

operation for one man to swing. Made this set-up look like a penny arcade."

"Interesting, huh? Mike and Adams in on a deal. Mike and Adams both get themselves dead."

"You think there's any connection?"

"I don't know. Two guys getting ready to move in on a deal to take over from the Havana boys. The Havana operation is run by Meyer Lansky. Meyer and Buggsy Siegel were once partners. Al Rossi used to run with the Bug and now Al Rossi is one of Mike's competitors. Could mean nothing, could mean plenty."

The deputy shook his head. "Mike and Rossi never saw eye to eye. Neither did Adams and Rossi. They never would have spilled to him."

"Maybe not, but who knows for sure? The only thing I am sure of now is that neither you nor Whitey had anything to gain from Fat Mike getting hit."

Thompson stared. "You mean you thought maybe I did it?"

Liddell grinned. "The thought had occurred to me," he conceded. "You won't forget to get me that gun, will you?"

"I won't forget." He stared at Liddell, shook his head. "How do you like a guy like this? I stick my neck all the way out for him and all the time he's trying to decide, whether to pin a killing on me or not."

"Don't take it so big. Some of my best friends are killers."

Thompson shook his head again, checked his watch. "I better get back. I'll manage to get the piece to you some way. How soon you figure you'll be needing it?"

"If I can have it by show time, it'll be fine."

Thompson bobbed his head. He walked to the door, opened it a crack, checked the hallway, then slipped out.

Liddell looked around the mess of the room with distaste. He made a desultory effort to straighten it up, gave up in disgust. Instead, he brushed some clothes off the chair, went rooting through the contents of the drawer, came up with a half-filled bottle and a glass, sat down to wait for the maid.

FIFTEEN

The first show of the evening at the Music Hall was at 8:30.

Johnny Liddell killed most of the late afternoon at the pool in a pair of trunks and sandals, a towel draped over his shoulders. He sat staring into the blue-green water of the pool, with the reflection of the white furniture in it. With a hot sun beating down on his shoulders, white cottony clouds suspended in space in the blue sky, the basement room at the County Courthouse and the dampness of the morgue seemed a long way off.

The sun was just showing signs of sinking below the horizon when Liddell heard his name being paged over the loud speaker. He signaled to a waiter, who brought a telephone to his table, plugged it in. "This is Liddell," he told the operator. "Were you paging me?"

"One moment, sir," the muted voice on the other end told him. Then, "Is this Mr. Johnny Liddell of Bungalow 8?"

"That's right."

"Would you come out to the desk, please? There's a package here for you."

"I'm at the pool in a bathing suit. Can you have it sent out to me?"

The operator hesitated for a moment. "Of course, Mr. Liddell," she said finally.

Liddell dropped the receiver back on its hook, the waiter came over, removed the phone.

"There's a package coming out from the desk. My name's Liddell. It's for me."

The waiter nodded, took the phone away.

A few minutes later, a uniformed deputy stood in the entrance to the flagstone terrace with a package in his hand. He looked around. The waiter walked up to him, pointed to where Liddell sat. The deputy nodded, walked over to him.

"Mr. Liddell?"

Liddell nodded.

The deputy handed over the package and a slip. "Will you sign for it, please?"

Johnny scribbled his name on the bottom of the slip, handed it back. He waited until the uniformed man had walked back into the casino, weighed the package in the flat of his hand. He got up, pulled the towel around his shoulders, headed up the grassy slope to his bungalow.

In his room, he tore the wrapper off the package. Inside was a snub-nosed .38 with a box of ammunition for it. He hefted the gun in the palm of his hand, liked the feel of it. It was lighter than his .45, but it packed undoubted authority. He loaded it, set it on top of the dresser, headed for the shower.

He had just finished toweling his damp hair when the telephone rang. He crossed from the bathroom to the night table, held the instrument to his ear. "Yeah?"

"Mr. Liddell?" It was Thompson's voice.

"Yes?"

"The desk has a package for you that came by Western Union. Have you received it?"

"Yes, thanks."

"Fine, sir. I thought it might be important and I didn't see you answer the page."

"I had it brought out to me at the pool. But thanks, anyway."

"You're very welcome, sir." There was a click as the receiver at the other end was dropped on its hook. Liddell listened for a moment, could detect no sign that the wire was open, replaced his instrument.

Liddell finished dressing, stuck the .38 in his waistband, checked his wristwatch. He had more than an hour to kill until the first show.

He started for the door, had his hand on the knob, when the phone started to jangle. He scowled, debated the advisability of ignoring it, lost the decision to his curiosity, he walked back, lifted the receiver to his ear.

"Liddell?" The voice had a familiar twang to it.

"Who's this?"

"Carl Jensen. From the Big Payoff. I thought maybe you'd have a drink with me before dinner."

Liddell frowned. "Where are you?"

"Your place. The Music Hall. In the bar."

Liddell hesitated for a moment, then answered, "I'll be right out."

"Fine." There was a click at the other end, the line went dead.

Liddell dropped his phone on the hook, scowled at it. Sommers was right. The kid was a hustler. He'd made the threat to Lewine to tip Fat Mike's friends that he'd been murdered. Now he was on the make for proof.

He tugged the .38 from his waistband, spun the cylinder. Tonight's payoff would answer a lot of questions.

130

But he had the unhappy feeling that Martin Sommers would not approve of his plans for the delivery.

Carl Jensen stood at the bar in the Music Hall, talking to a tall brunette, as Johnny Liddell walked in. She was a few inches taller than Jensen, wore her dark hair flat across her head, a dozen or more strands pasted diagonally across her forehead à la Juliette Greco. She had the well-cared-for body of a dancer, a waist almost thin enough to be spanned by a man's hands.

The low cut of her neckline emphasized the deep hollow between her breasts and served to accentuate their prominence and perfect roundness. She smiled tentatively as Liddell walked up, joined them.

"Turn off the come-on, babe," Jensen snapped at her. "Go comb your hair or something. I've got business with this guy."

He added something under his breath that Johnny Liddell missed. Liddell thought he caught a quick flash of resentment in the girl's eyes. She merely smiled, however, patted the thick glistening black coils that were caught up in a knot at the nape of her neck and rose to her feet.

Jensen watched the supple figure as it moved across the room, finally brought his attention back to Liddell.

"Have a drink?"

"Scotch on the rocks."

Jensen passed the order along to the bartender, turned back to Liddell. "That was a pretty good tip you gave me last night, Liddell." He picked up the drink in front of him, swirled it around the glass. "I guess you knew what you were talking about."

Liddell raised his eyebrows. "Which one was that?"

The man with the pocked face smiled tolerantly.

"Look, this is just between you and me. You can level." He waited while the bartender slid the scotch across the bar. As soon as the man behind the stick moved down the bar, Jensen continued, "Adams and Fat Mike were murdered all right." He watched Liddell take a deep swallow from his glass. "How much would it cost for the proof?"

Liddell sighed. "There is no proof. Adams was cremated and Fat Mike is embalmed. Both death certificates are on file—one heart attack, one suicide."

Jensen ignored the statement. "I can get fifty gees for my share of the Big Payoff."

Liddell shook his head. "I just told you—"

"Seventy-five," Jensen cut him off. He studied Liddell's face. "I'll go to a hundred. And that's it." He leaned over to Johnny, dropped his voice. "I need proof, Liddell. With proof I can parlay this into a million. Without it, I'm stymied."

"Benny Lewine?"

. Jensen shrugged, straightened up. "For a start. Look, a guy like me, this town is made to take. But you need a gimmick. Give me that proof, Liddell, that's all the gimmick I need."

Across the room, the brunette had left the powder room. Jensen saw her, swore under his breath. He pulled a memo book from his pocket, scribbled his name and address on a sheet, tore it out and passed it to Liddell.

"If you change your mind—"

Liddell was listening with only half an ear. He was watching the progress of the girl across the room, contemplating the unfairness of the fact that the voluptuous type always turns to fat. He sighed, comforted himself with the thought that until they do—

Jensen scowled irritably as his eyes followed the mag-

132

net for Liddell's attention. He wasn't used to people listening to him with half an ear. Even when he was asking them to do him a favor.

"Look, Liddell. You dig the babe that much, I'll throw her in for a bonus."

Liddell reluctantly tore his eyes from the jiggling progress of the girl, focused his eyes on the man alongside him. "If I come up with the proof, I might just take you up on that." He moved back, made room for the girl at the bar. She thanked him with her eyes. Jensen glowered. "There's nothing like incentive pay to make a man really do his best. And they can't even tax that kind."

The first show of the evening was in full swing in the Music Hall when Johnny Liddell walked in. The dinner room, set off from the casino, was built along the lines of an amphitheater. The dance floor was bathed by hidden spots, nestled at the foot of tiered rows of tables that rose in sharp ascent. There was no ceiling to the two-story annex; a sliding top covered the entire area in the unlikely event of rain.

On the floor, a group of chorines was making a half-hearted effort to keep time to the brassy rhythm of the orchestra. They scampered around, bare legs flashing, stomachs undulating. Behind them, on small pedestals, the show girls stood motionless, their breasts bared to the spotlights.

Liddell squinted into the amphitheater, noted that most of the tables were filled. A fat man in a midnight-blue tuxedo walked over to him.

"You have a reservation, sir?" His pudgy fingers fumbled with the red carnation in his buttonhole, his wet lips glistened in the semigloom.

"My name's Liddell. I think a reservation was made for me by Mr. Sommers?"

The headwaiter's head bobbed unctuously, disturbing the rolls of fat under his chin. "Yes, indeed, Mr. Liddell. We've been expecting you." He snapped his fingers, scowled at the time it took a captain to bring over a menu. He selected a leather-bound copy, turned and led the way down the incline toward the ringside tables.

Some of the tables were occupied by faces Johnny recognized from the Sunday supplements, others from their packages at various Police Headquarters. It was a typical audience for a house on the Hood Circuit—café society and Hollywood mixed in equal parts with the underworld, spiced with a sprinkling of tourists.

As usual the beauty of the girls at the hoods' tables was in direct ratio to the size of the hoods' package at headquarters. Just as the length of a Cadillac is the status symbol of society, the beauty and price tag of the girl a man wears on his arm is the status symbol of the underworld.

Along the way, Liddell nodded to a couple of ringsiders who favored him with looks that showed no signs of enthusiasm. One of them he had helped to send away for a five-year stretch from which he had recently been paroled. The other had once harbored the notion that he could take Liddell in a no-holds-barred contest. The curious twist to his nose was the only visible evidence that he had been wrong. Both men got very interested in the conversation at their table as Liddell walked by.

The chorus line was running off the floor and the spots blacked out, leaving the stage in darkness. The headwaiter stopped alongside a table near the orchestra, Liddell whispered an order for a scotch and soda, sat down at the table.

The chorus line was followed by a dance duo. They handled their routines with consummate grace, but from where Liddell sat it was obvious that the male's teeth were too white and the female didn't have enough meat on her to make a good soup. Several times, during their closing adagio number, Liddell winced, fearing that the male would be impaled on one of her protruding hip bones..

After two encores, one of which was legitimate, the dance team ran to the backstage exit and the lights went down again. This time an opaque curtain swung around the stage, obscuring it completely. The master of ceremonies stepped out of the curtain, stood in the spotlight, rubbing his hands, counting the house. He launched into a long topical routine that had borrowed generously from Mort Sahl and Shelley Berman with a soupçon of Jonathan Winters. The result was a sickly take-off on sick comedians. He seemed unperturbed by the audience's lack of enthusiasm, closed with a one-sided telephone bit that hammered home *double-entendres* with the sublety of a sledge hammer.

Johnny Liddell sighed, ordered another drink, consoled himself with the knowledge that a way of making a living without occupational hazards such as this has yet to be discovered.

When the curtain rolled back, he felt compensated for what he had just been forced to sit through. A huge bathtub dominated the stage, two girls were scampering around in abbreviated maids' costumes. The band swung into a slow, sensuous rendition of "Lady of the Evening." The spot shot to the corner of the band stand, picked up a tall blonde in an iridescent blue gown. Her hair was piled on top of her head.

135

As she strutted in, the two girls poured liquid bubble bath into the tub.

The blonde smiled at each of the girls, started across the floor to a large mirror. As she walked, she managed to give her body a rhythm that started her breasts flowing and swaying in the loose bodice of her gown. She stood in front of the mirror, stripping off her long gloves. Then she reached up and pulled off her earrings.

Now the orchestra stepped up its tempo. She half danced, half strutted across the floor, unzipping her gown as she walked to a screen. By the time she reached it, the dress hung open to the waist, her breasts bobbing in and out of it like something alive. At the screen, she stepped behind it, threw the dress over the top.

When she walked from behind the screen, the whiteness of her body gleamed in the spotlight. Her legs were long, sensuously shaped. Full, rounded thighs swelled into high-set hips and converged into a narrow waist. A thin brassière made a half-hearted attempt to restrain the tip-tilted breasts, a beaded fringe hung from her hips.

The drummer, his face gleaming with sweat, his lips moving spasmodically, started to add a primitive beat that stood the hairs on Liddell's neck on end.

The blonde walked over to the tub, undulated sensuously. Her hands hung at her sides. Then they came up slowly, the palms smoothing the skin on her hips, over her stomach, to cup her breasts. Her shoulders picked up the rhythm of the drum. She reached up into her hair, turned it loose to stream down in a molten cascade over her shoulders. The room became charged with electricity as the blonde stood, feet rooted to the floor, her movements becoming more and more abandoned in time to the music. Finally, the music hit a shattering peak of rimshots, dropped away. The blonde stood for a moment, tore away the net brassière.

136

Quickly the maids maneuvered oversized towels between her and the audience. She wrapped one around her, wiggled a little, and the beaded fringe that hung from her hips fell to the floor. She walked to the tub, tested it with a toe, shuddered deliciously. With her back to the audience, she lowered the towel slowly, stepped into the tub. Finally the towel dropped away completely as she slid down into the bubbles.

One shapely leg protruded from the bubbles, and the blonde massaged it sensuously with both hands. She repeated the process with the other leg.

Liddell looked around. The faces at ringside were white blobs, glistening wetly in the reflected light.

The blonde started to stand up, the maids sprang into position with outspread towel. Behind it, the blonde reached up, wiggled as she ran her fingers through her hair. She took the towel from the girls, wrapped it around her.

Suddenly the towel fell away, she stood for a moment, her body clothed in nothing but patches of heavy bubbles. She screamed, turned and ran for the exit, shedding oily bubbles behind her. Once behind the backstage curtain, she refused to be coaxed out for an encore. She stuck her leg out, kicked it twice in appreciation of the applause, then she was gone.

The lights went down, the heavy curtain circled the stage. While two stagehands were maneuvering a piano through the curtain, a waiter materialized alongside Liddell's table.

"Quite a dish," Liddell commented.

"All woman." The waiter wiped his forehead with his sleeve. "I watch her like twice a night for seven nights a week and she still gets to me."

"I thought there was a new show tonight."

The waiter grinned tightly. "Only the headliner. This

137

one goes with the lease." He looked around, lowered his voice. "Her man packs a lot of weight in this town, so if you had any ideas you better plan on peddling your sex life somewhere else. He don't like competition."

Liddell raised his eyebrows, managed to look impressed. "Thanks for the tip."

The waiter shrugged. "Why ask for trouble? You want a girl, the town's full of them. All sizes, all shades, all prices. Now, I know a kid—"

Liddell shook his head. "No, thanks."

The waiter shrugged. "I been in this town a long time, buddy. Take my word for it. Cold turkey may not be as spicy as chili—but a guy's less likely to get burned. You know?" He glanced at the preparations being made onstage. "If you want another drink, I'd better get it before the closing number."

Liddell nodded. "The same."

A hidden orchestra swung into the opening strains of a torch song. Lee Loomis stepped out onto the far rim of the stage, was picked up by a spotlight as she walked toward the piano. The walk was a production in itself. She was wearing a black décolleté dress that clung to her ample curves like a wet bathing suit.

The waiters stopped their endless prowling, the murmur of conversation died away as the spotlight pinned her to the piano. There was a wave of applause, then the audience settled back expectantly.

The redhead listened while her accompanist fingered the introduction to the torch song, her eyes roamed the big room. From where she stood, the upper tables looked like fireflies as their candles flickered in the breeze. Suddenly, as her eyes moved along the ringside tables, she saw Liddell, smiled at him.

The rest of the orchestra picked up the accompanist's

beat, the redhead swayed to the rhythm of the music. Her voice, when she sang, was husky, throbbing, played on the backbone like a xylophone. She directed the song toward Liddell, as if he were the only one there. He leaned back, enjoyed the pleasant things she was doing to the number.

Suddenly it was over. The audience expressed its approval with waves of applause increasing in volume to a thunderous roar.

She did two more blues numbers that brought the house down, closed with "Who's Sorry Now?" At the end of "Sorry," she broke for the wings. The thunderous applause followed her. She shook her head at cries for "More! More!" permitted herself to be drawn back onstage. She raised her hand for attention, the roar subsided.

"I'd love to do more, folks, but we have another show at 12:30. The casino is open and waiting for you. So good night, and good luck."

The floor lights went down, the house lights went up. The curtain around the stage remained closed, the two stagehands were struggling with the piano.

The rumble of conversation, the jingling of glasses and silverware that had died away during Lee Loomis's turn were back. The contest was now on for the girls at the various tables to vie for attention. Some of them did it by heading for the powder room with an exaggerated swing of their hips that started their breasts swaying, threatening to spill out of their low-cut dresses. Others table-hopped, hoping their wide acquaintance would be noticed by the columnists who had turned out for the opening.

The tourists were easily identifiable. They were already on their feet, pushing and shoving in their eagerness to

139

get back into the casinos to leave a bigger share of their holdings.

Johnny Liddell checked his watch, found it nearly ten, wondered idly how the contact would be made. He shook a cigarette loose from his pack, tapped it on the corner of his table. He lit it and settled back to wait.

SIXTEEN

Johnny Liddell was on his second cigarette when he saw Whitey, Fat Mike's former casino boss turned successor, standing at the entrance, talking to the headwaiter. He saw the fat man point down to where he sat. Whitey looked in his direction, started down to him.

He stopped alongside Liddell's table, tossed a small cardboard square bearing the number 32 in front of him. "There's a package in the checkroom for you, shamus. Marty Sommers sent it over. Said you expected it." He stared down at Liddell with no show of enthusiasm. "We could use that room of yours. Hope you're not figuring on being around too long."

Liddell picked up the checkroom stub, dropped it into his pocket. "I'll tell you when I'm ready to leave."

Whitey scowled down at him. "I don't like you, shamus. I don't like anything about you. Including your friends." He tossed his head in the direction of the casino. "I saw you in there with Jensen and his broad. Meet your friends some place else. You'll be giving the joint a bad name." He squinted at Liddell. "Like I said, we can use the room—"

"Look, friend, don't go looking for grief. Fat Mike

141

brought me out here to do a job for him. He has a lot of friends in New York who might get curious about why you don't want that job done."

Whitey tried to match Liddell's stare, dropped his eyes. "I don't know anything about what he brought you out here for."

"Then don't go buying trouble trying to stop me from finishing it."

Whitey started to retort, changed his mind, turned around and headed back up the stairs.

Liddell chain-lit a fresh cigarette from the butt between his fingers. His watch showed 10:05 and he was conscious of a feeling of tense anticipation. He wondered what the mechanics of the payoff would be and what steps the extortionist would take to guard against a double-cross. He hoped the shake artist would be counting heavily enough on his victims' fear not to take too many precautions.

Slowly the dining room emptied. By 10:30 there were only three tables besides his own occupied. At the door, the fat man in the blue tuxedo was busily checking his reservation lists for the next show. A couple of waiters leaned against the wall with checks in their hands, waiting for an opportune time to present them.

"You, Mr. Liddell?" A thin old man in a blue lightweight suit stood alongside his table, a stained fedora in his hand.

Liddell nodded, crushed out his cigarette. "Got a message for me, Pop?"

"Harry's the name, mister," the old man whined. "I'm the doorman backstage." He looked around, dropped his voice. "Lee Loomis wants to see you. In her dressing room."

Liddell let his breath out in a low whistle. He fumbled in his pocket, separated a bill from the roll replenished by a cashed check. He shoved it into the old man's hand. "Okay, Pop. I'll be right back."

"Harry," the old man reminded him patiently.

"Okay, Harry."

He waited until the old man had disappeared through the door leading backstage. Then he flagged down his waiter, settled his bill. He fumbled through his pockets, came up with the checkroom stub.

"Will you get this out of the checkroom and bring it back to Miss Loomis's dressing room?" He handed him the stub, added a five-dollar bill. "Give me five minutes or so before you bring it back. Okay?"

The waiter smoothed out the bill, leered. "Just five minutes?"

Liddell crossed the dance floor to the door leading to backstage, pushed through. The old man sat at a small table near a door leading out behind the casino area. There were two coffee-stained containers on the table in front of him. He pulled a blackened briar from between his teeth, pointed with the stem. "Third dressing room on the right-hand side."

Liddell headed down the narrow corridor. A door opened on the left side, the blonde who had done the bathtub number stepped out. Her face was a dark tan, glistened with an oil makeup, her mouth was a crimson slash. Her blonde hair was almost white in the corridor light.

"I liked your act," Liddell told her.

She looked him over with frank interest. "You should see what I do for an encore."

"That an invitation?"

The blonde shrugged. "Why don't you try taking me up on it?"

"Maybe I will. But if I did, I couldn't just go asking for the chocolate dish with the white frosting."

"Try asking for Maisie." The sensuous lips twisted in a grin. "That is, if you're not worried about my boy friend. He's kind of jealous."

"Would I know this boy friend?"

The eyes looked him over appraisingly. She shrugged. "Your type might. He's the sheriff."

Liddell raised his eyebrows. "That could stunt a girl's social life."

The blonde considered it, shrugged. "Not necessarily. It depends on the man. The risk makes it all the more interesting."

Liddell grinned. "I see what you mean."

The blonde made no move to step back into her room as he started past. He had to brush against her, had a fleeting impression of a well-rounded breast and thigh. Her perfume was heavy, heady. She watched him until he stopped outside Lee Loomis's door.

"One thing I have to give those redheads," she told him with an amused smile. "They sure manage to do all right for themselves." She jabbed at her hair with her fingertips. "I think I'll go back to being one."

Liddell knocked at the door, Lee Loomis tugged it open. She looked from him to the blonde leaning against the corridor wall. "Don't mind Maisie, Johnny. She can't break the habit of standing outside the door, displaying the merchandise." She grabbed him by the arm, pulled him inside and slammed the door, cutting off the blonde's retort.

Lee grinned at Liddell. "I know it's bitchy, but that Rexall snow-top brings it out in me. You should have heard the hassle today. That pin-up for a Peeping Tom had the guts to yell for top billing."

Liddell shrugged. "You've got to admit she does have talent."

"It takes talent to take off your clothes? You want to

144

see a naked woman, the galleries and museums are full of them. When you've seen one naked woman, you've seen them all."

"The waiter tells me she's been here like forever."

The redhead snorted. "Because she's the original good time that's been had by all. Latest is the sheriff. He's got more brothers-in-law in this town than you could shake a stick at." The frown faded off her face, was replaced by a grin. "It sure gave me a lift to look around and see you out there, Johnny."

"I told you I'd be here."

"I didn't expect you for the first show."

Liddell stuck a cigarette between his lips, touched a match to it. "To tell you the truth, I didn't expect to catch the first show. I was out front on business."

The redhead picked the cigarette from between his lips, took a deep drag. "What kind of business?"

"You tell me."

Lee Loomis stared at him, replaced the cigarette between his lips. "What's that mean?"

"I was supposed to sit out front until someone made contact. You made contact." He scowled at her. "Don't you have some instructions for me?"

She turned, reached over onto the cluttered dressing table. "I sent Harry out to get you because he brought this in to me. It was tacked to the call-board backstage."

The envelope had Lee Loomis's name on it. Inside it was another envelope and a folded sheet of paper. It was the same cheap, untraceable paper on which the extortion notes had been written.

The note addressed to the redhead read:

Johnny Liddell will be sitting ringside at your first show. Give him the enclosed. It is very important.

145

Liddell took the second envelope, tore it open. The message was short and to the point:

> *Be on Flight 112 leaving 11:30 from Las Palmas to Los Angeles. Further instructions your name Western Union office in L.A. airport. You're being watched. Don't try anything or the price goes up again and one of the boys won't like it.*

Liddell read the note twice, swore softly under his breath. He wondered if the instructions in Los Angeles would be to continue on to Tia Juana. The more he thought about it, the more convinced he was that the shake and the Tia Juana operation were connected in some way.

The redhead picked the note from between Johnny's fingers, read it. "What's it mean?"

Liddell studied her face. "What does Tia Juana mean to you?"

The redhead puzzled over it, shrugged. "A good place to stay away from. It's wide open. Girls, dope, gambling. You name it and, for a price, you've got it."

"What's your price, baby?"

Lee Loomis stared at him, slack-jawed. "My price?"

"Fat Mike was getting ready to walk away from Las Palmas. He and Larry Adams were getting set to open up in Tia Juana. You didn't know about that, I suppose?"

The redhead shook her head. "No."

"Adams and Mike were put on the spot. For a price."

The girl shook her head slowly as though she had difficulty believing what she heard. "You don't think I—"

Liddell scowled at her. "Maybe Mike was getting set to dump you. You said yourself Whitey wouldn't look you over like a side of beef if he knew what was good

146

for him. Maybe he already had the flash Mike was dump-
ing you—"

"Or maybe he wasn't afraid of what Mike would do
because he already knew Mike was dead. You ever think
of that?"

Liddell nodded. "I thought of it. Only Whitey stood
nothing to gain and a lot to lose if Mike was murdered.
Mike's friends might send some boys in here asking
questions. With Mike alive, Whitey was getting the casino with no strings. Maybe you with it."

"That's crazy, Johnny. I swear to you there was nothing between Mike and me. He just liked to show me off,
make people think—"

She started nervously at the knock on the door.

Liddell put his finger to his lips, motioned for her to
open the door. She waited until he had stepped back out
of sight, walked over and pulled the door partially open.

A waiter stood in the corridor, a valise in his hand.
He eyed the redhead with appreciation. "A customer
asked me to deliver this to your dressing room, Miss
Loomis. That okay?"

The girl managed to nod her head, stood aside while
he deposited the valise inside the door. She thanked him
with a wan smile, closed the door behind him. She looked
from Liddell to the bag and back.

"What is it, Johnny?"

"A million bucks, baby." Liddell stepped to the door,
satisfied himself that the corridor was deserted. The
waiter stood gossiping with the old man at the stage
door. "That's the package I'm to take to L.A." He knelt
alongside the valise, tried the catches. They were locked.
He looked up into the white face of the redhead. "A million bucks," he repeated. "Don't hardly see nothing like
that no more, do you?" He stood up, brushed the dust
from his knee.

"You going to give that to them?"

"Why not? It's not my money." He crushed out the cigarette, watched the smoke spiral slowly upward from the ash tray. "They want to contribute a cool million to some shake artist, they can be my guest."

The redhead put her hand on his arm. "Be careful, Johnny."

Liddell grinned at her. "That a warning or advice?"

"Both. I told you before—they're mad dogs. They won't think anything of shooting you down after they've used you."

"I don't think so much of the idea myself."

The redhead wagged her head. "I'm serious, Johnny. I'm scared for you, taking chances like this."

"It all shows up on the bill."

"I don't care about the bill. I don't care about anything except you coming back." She came to him, slid her arms around his neck. "Come back for me, Johnny." She reached up, pasted her lips against his.

After a moment, they broke, he held her out at arm's length. Her breasts were heaving, her mouth moist and half parted, the slanted eyes were heavy lidded.

"You will come back for me?" she asked huskily.

"I'll be back."

She moved into his arms, tilted her head, lifted her mouth to be kissed.

"Just turn on half the juice this time, baby," Liddell told her. "I'm flying to L.A. but I had in mind something with wings."

He closed his lips down on hers.

SEVENTEEN

Johnny Liddell sat in the passenger lounge of the South-western Airlines at the Las Palmas Airport, the locked valise at his feet. He checked his ticket, nodded his satisfaction at the name Ralph Chase in the box marked *Passenger's Name*. He returned it to his pocket, stole a glance at his watch. The flight to L.A. was due to start loading in a matter of minutes.

Liddell stood up, stretched and looked around. None of the other occupants of the lounge seemed to be paying him any undue attention. He picked up his valise, walked to the men's room.

The loudspeaker boomed from the wall. "Flight 112, nonstop to Los Angeles loading on Ramp 3. All passengers for Flight 112 please go to Ramp 3."

Liddell walked to the door, opened it a crack. The other occupants of the lounge were obediently trickling toward the door opening onto the field singly and in pairs. No one seemed to be aware that he was still in the men's room. When the last passenger had left the lounge, Liddell closed the door.

"Will passenger Ralph Chase please report to Ramp 3?" the loudspeaker boomed a few minutes later.

Liddell waited, checked his watch. Three minutes

later, the announcement was repeated over the loud-speaker. He looked out into the lounge. It was completely empty.

"Flight 112 leaving on schedule at 11:30. Will passenger Ralph Chase please report?"

Liddell checked his watch, waited until the minute hand was on the half hour, then watched it crawl to the 7. There was no further call for passenger Chase. He gave it another three minutes, then picked up his bag and walked out into the lounge. A sleepy-eyed porter, gathering up the newspapers left around the room by the recently departed passengers gave him an incurious glance, went back to his work.

Johnny carried the valise to the entrance of the lounge, looked out. The Southwestern counter men were busily checking in passengers for the Las Palmas–New Orleans flight at 12:15. Men lugging suitcases, women carrying children or sleepy-eyed from marathon stretches in the casinos, stood lined up, watching the airline clerks behind the counter going through their paces.

Liddell walked out of the lounge, melted into the crowds clustered around the counter. He stayed in line long enough to satisfy himself no one was watching him. Then, picking up the valise, he headed for the exit leading to the parking field and his rented car.

It was not yet twelve when he came in sight of the lights of the Strip drenching the sky with multicolored brilliance. He pulled over to the side of the road, cut his motor, doused his lights.

Ten minutes later, satisfied that he had not been followed, he got out of the car, tugged the valise from the back seat.

The sand seemed glued to his feet, made his shoes feel like hundred-pound weights as he walked his burden back into the desert. He passed a clump of trees and underbrush about a hundred yards from the road, kept going. Once he stumbled over a root, almost dropped the valise. He swore, wiped the perspiration out of his eyes and kept going. When he estimated that he was about three hundred yards from the road, he set the valise down, swabbed his streaming face on his sleeve. His heart was pounding in his chest, his breath was beginning to get short. He sat on the valise for a moment, then as soon as he caught his breath, he got to his knees, started scooping a hole in the sand.

Fifteen minutes later, satisfied with the hole, he placed the valise in it, started covering it with sand. By the time he was finished, the valise was buried from twelve to fourteen inches deep. He swabbed at his face again, started back to where he had left the car. Once there, he sank back against the cushions, leaned his head on the back of the seat, caught his breath.

His wristwatch showed 12:10.

Finally seated, he turned the key in the ignition, snapped on his brights and stamped the motor into roaring life. The business day in Las Palmas was just beginning and Liddell had laid out a full night's work for himself.

The clock on the wall in the sheriff's office showed midnight. He sat frowning at the solitaire layout on the top of his desk, riffled through the cards in the pack, tossed them down on the desk in disgust. He rummaged through the butts in the ash tray at his elbow, came up with a half-smoked one, stuck it in the corner of his mouth, lit it.

He had collected the cards, started a new deal when the door to the office opened and Ted Linehan walked in. The sheriff scowled his annoyance.

"What'd you get from him?"

Linehan shrugged. "Nothing. Because he don't know nothing. He's down there crying like a baby. Anything he knew he would've spilled long ago."

Regan threw the cards down on the desk, swore under his breath. He picked up the phone, dialed a number.

"Bauer? This is the sheriff. Get over here right away."

Without waiting for an answer, he dropped the receiver on its hook, looked up at Linehan. "He marked up?"

The big man shrugged. "Some. Not too bad."

"Don't mark him up any more. Go down and keep him company until I call for you."

He watched the bulky-shouldered man walk out of the office, slam the door behind him. Then Regan got up, walked to the window, stared out. When he took cards in the game he had no idea the stakes were going to be so high. But he was in too deep now to try to get out. He wondered if Tia Juana was going to be as good as it was cracked up to be, admitted glumly to himself that he was in a helluva spot to find out.

He walked over to the water cooler that was humming to itself against the wall, helped himself to a drink. One thing he wasn't going to miss on leaving Las Palmas was the brackish taste of its water. He threw out most of it, crumpled the cup and tossed it at the wastebasket. After tonight all the loose ends would be tied up and he could start severing his connections with Las Palmas. He wished the dawn light wouldn't drag on the way it was. For the tenth time since 11:30, he looked up at the wall clock, checked it against his wristwatch to make sure it hadn't stopped.

Regan was pacing the office nervously when the door opened and Larry Bauer walked in. "What's the fever?" he wanted to know.

152

The sheriff walked around his desk, dropped into his chair. "Got a job for you." He pulled open his bottom drawer, took out a .45, laid it on the desk. "This is the gun you took out of Liddell's room. I want you to use it."

"On who?"

Regan peered at him, pursed his lips. "Not that it's any of your business but it's a character named Jensen. He owns a piece of a joint on Front Street. He's got a fatal case of ambition." He pushed the gun across the desk. "He's been seen talking to Liddell tonight. Could be they were arguing." He twisted his features into a scowl. "There was a broad with them. She'll testify anything I tell her to."

Bauer bobbed his head. "Jensen gets hit with Liddell's gun, they've been arguing." He considered it, approved. "Sounds okay."

"I want it real clean," Regan growled. "I'm calling the state cops in on it. I want them to check the bullet out. I want them to verify it's Liddell's gun."

"And what's the shamus going to be doing when you pin this on him?"

"Leave him to me. I'll take care of him when the time comes."

Bauer shrugged. He picked up the gun, weighed it in the palm of his hand. "Where do I find this Jensen?"

"You don't have to. We have him on ice." He got up, led the way to the door, then down the stairs to the basement.

Carl Jensen was sitting on the wooden chair. He was no longer dapper. The carefully-combed hair hung lankly down over his face, his chin was supported by his chest.

Regan walked over to where Jensen sat. He caught him by the tie, pulled him to his feet. "You just got

153

lucky, Jensen," the white-haired man told him. "The operators decided to go easy. You just get to stay out of town."

The man with the pocked face licked at his lips, rolled his eyes up to the sheriff's face. "Okay, I know when I'm licked."

Regan nodded his head. "Now you're being smart." He motioned to the sink and mirror. "Get yourself fixed up."

Jensen tottered over to the sink, ran the cold tap over his head. Then he took a comb from his hip pocket, combed the dark hair into place. He dried his face on a towel, tried to brush some of the creases out of his clothes. He turned slowly.

"Look, Sheriff, maybe we can make a deal. Maybe I could make it more worth your while than Lewine if you throw in with me—" He studied the hard expression on Regan's face, shook his head. "No, I guess not. Okay. I'll get out."

The sheriff nodded to Linehan. "You'd better make sure to pick up the other guy on your way."

Bauer said, "I'll take care of that, Sheriff. Linehan can be responsible for this one. I'll take the other." He tugged open the heavy door, waited until Linehan had escorted his prisoner through. He turned, nodded to the sheriff. "I'll take good care of it." He followed Linehan, left the sheriff standing in the basement room alone.

Johnny Liddell parked the car in the lot behind Bungalow 8, merged into the shadows and headed for the rear exit of his building. There was no sign of life near the bungalow, he made it in the rear door with no trouble.

Inside the corridor, he fitted his key to the lock, pushed open the door. He wrinkled his nose at the familiar odor of cordite, swore softly and closed the door

154

behind him. The chair in the center of the room had been overturned, the desk lamp lay on the floor.

A pair of legs extended from behind the couch. He crossed to the body, turned it over. Carl Jensen stared up at him with dead eyes. A heavy, soggy stain on the front of his shirt hadn't yet begun to darken. The skin on the side of his face was still warm to the touch.

Liddell checked his watch. 12:45.

He started to straighten up when he saw the butt of a gun sticking out from under the couch. He reached over, picked it up, turned it over from side to side. There was no doubt in his mind that the .45 that had disappeared from his closet had mysteriously reappeared. And from the size of the holes in the dead man's chest, it didn't take a Sherlock Holmes to guess that the slugs in Jensen came from his gun.

"A nice picture with frame to match and me sitting dead center," he growled. He straightened up, looked around. There was nothing else out of place, no other "clues."

He put the lamp back on the desk, stood the chair up. Then he caught the body under the arms, dragged it to the closet. He wrestled it to its feet, propped it in a standing position deep in the closet, hooked its collar onto a coat hook to assure its standing back out of sight.

He crossed quickly to the telephone, dialed operator.

"Number please?"

"Connect me with the backstage doorman at the supper club."

"One moment, please." There was a slight delay, then the sound of a receiver being lifted.

"Backstage."

"Harry?"

"Who's this?"

"Liddell. You brought me back to Lee Loomis's room

155

after the first show. Remember?" Without waiting for the old man's reply, he plunged ahead. "What time does the last show end tonight?"

He could hear the old man sucking on the pipe, rattling the juices in its stem. "One-thirty. You want to leave a message for—"

Liddell shook his head. "No. I want to surprise her. Don't say anything about my calling."

"Whatever you say." From his tone, it was obvious the old man didn't hold with such nonsense. "Anything else?"

"Not right now. I'll catch up with you tomorrow night."

"Okay." He sounded mollified as he hung up.

Liddell walked to the closet, brought out his shoulder harness. He stripped off his jacket, shrugged into the harness, covered it again with the jacket. He picked up the .45, checked the magazine, found that four bullets had been fired. He dropped the old magazine into a drawer, replaced it with a fresh magazine. He stuck the .45 in its hammock, welcomed the familiar weight under his arm.

His watch said 1:15.

He locked the door to the closet, dropped the key into his pocket. Then, walking to the hall door, he snapped off the lights, opened the door and peered up the hall. An elderly woman in a maid's uniform with some sheets folded over her arm was headed down the hall in his direction.

He eased the door closed, snapped on the lights. It couldn't take more than fifteen minutes for the woman to finish making up whatever room she was heading for—

There was a rap on the door, a pause, then Liddell heard a key being fitted to the lock. He hesitated for a moment, then grabbed the knob, pulled the door open.

He looked into the startled face of the housekeeper.

"I'm sorry. I didn't know anyone was in there." She looked past him, frowned at the sight of the made bed, looked back to Liddell. "Didn't you call for fresh linen?"

Liddell looked back to the bed, shook his head. "I didn't." He walked back to the bed, pulled down the spread. The pillow cases and sheets were immaculate.

The housekeeper dug into her pocket, brought up a slip, checked it against the number of the room. "I'm sorry, sir. Those girls can't get anything right." She squinted at the penciled notation again. "This is the room they gave me. Said the gentleman was complaining something fierce." She sighed, shook her head. "I guess we'll be hearing from him again." She turned, waddled toward the exit at the end of the hall.

Liddell wiped at the tiny beads of perspiration on his upper lip with the back of his hand. It had been cut too close for comfort. Someone had arranged for Jensen to be killed with Liddell's gun in Liddell's room. Then that someone had conveniently arranged to have a house-keeper walk in on the dead man and give the alarm. It had been cut much too close!

He walked out into the hall, closed the door behind him. Instead of heading for the front entrance to the building, he went out the back door again, headed for his car in the parking lot, settled down to wait.

EIGHTEEN

Johnny Liddell sat huddled behind the wheel of his car, held his cigarette cupped in the palm of his hand. He took a deep drag, blew the smoke at the floorboard.

The last time he had looked at his watch, it had been 1:40. Already some of the showgirls had come out of the stage door of the Music Hall supper club, had disappeared in the direction of their bungalows. He took another drag on his cigarette, then flipped the butt through the open window.

The Las Palmas–Los Angeles plane was due to land at 3:30. By now, he should be halfway to the payoff. He shifted uncomfortably, wondered whether or not he had played his hand the right way.

Suddenly he stiffened. A big black Buick with the words *Sheriff, Las Palmas, Nevada* had pulled up outside of the stage door. The door on the driver's side opened, the white hair of the sheriff glistened in the half light. He walked to the stage door, disappeared inside.

Johnny Liddell stepped on his starter, waited.

It took the sheriff less than ten minutes to reappear. He had the blonde with him, they appeared to be arguing. Regan pushed her roughly into the front seat, slammed the door, stalked around to his side. He raced his motor with a roar, swung in a U-turn and headed for the highway.

Liddell let him get a reasonable lead, snapped on his lights and proceeded to follow.

The sheriff was a fast driver, paid little heed to traffic regulations. But traffic was light enough so that Liddell had no difficulty in keeping the other car's taillight in sight.

Regan was heading north on the Las Palmas highway in the direction of the Las Palmas airport. He passed through Restaurant Row without decreasing his speed noticeably, headed for the residential area beyond. About six miles north of the Strip, his rear lights blinked on as he braked the car preparatory to swinging off the road onto a driveway that was hidden by high hedges.

Liddell slowed down, was doing under forty as he rolled past the entrance to the driveway. The big Buick was parked on the apron of a circular driveway that led to a sprawling ranch type house with a white tile roof.

The car door was open, the interior lights spilled out onto the driveway. The sheriff was standing at the open door, apparently still arguing with the blonde, making his points by pounding his fist against the heel of his hand.

Liddell rolled the car past, pulled to the side of the road under a big tree about a quarter of a mile beyond the driveway. He doused his lights, settled down to wait. When the Buick didn't roll out in fifteen minutes, he decided the sheriff was settled for the night.

He pulled his car farther off the road, deeper into the shadows of the tree. Then he got out, trudged back the quarter of a mile, staying as far off the road as possible. Once when a car rocketed by on its way from the airport toward the Strip, he flattened himself against an embankment, waited until the car had become no more than a cone of light in the distance.

At the entrance to the driveway he debated the advisability of going over the hedge, decided it might be electrified. Instead, he sidled around the hedge, entered the driveway.

There were no lights on in the front of the house. The Buick had apparently been driven into the garage, the doors closed. Liddell kept in the shadows, walked to the side of the house. He could see a large patch of light on the back lawn indicating that some of the rooms in the rear were lighted. He followed the side of the garage to the rear, his hand on the butt of his .45.

In the backyard he continued to hug the shadows, worked his way around a small fishpool to a sheltering clump of hemlock that gave the yard full privacy from the rear.

The light came from a large picture window in what was obviously a family room or den. Alongside the window French doors opened onto the patio that overlooked the fish pool.

Through the window, Liddell had a perfect view of Tom Regan pouring himself a stiff drink of straight liquor. The sheriff lifted it to his lips, tossed it off with a grimace.

The door to the room opened, the blonde walked in. She had substituted a red dressing gown for the wrap she had worn out of the stage door. She walked to a large mirror, proceeded to brush her long hair, her back to the sheriff.

Regan said something to her, the girl gave no sign that she heard. She continued to run the brush through her hair.

The sheriff crossed the room to where she stood,

160

caught her by the arm and spun her around. He snarled something at her, her face contorted with anger as she spat her defiance back at him.

He brought his hand back, slashed the flat of his hand against her cheek, knocking her head to one side. He backhanded it into position. The blonde put the back of her hand against the side of her cheek, backed away from him, still spitting abuse at him. Regan reached out, caught her robe, yanked her to him.

Suddenly, the night air was rent with a loud explosion that lighted the sky to the north with the brilliance of day. It knocked Liddell to his knees, almost caused him to drop his gun. Inside the house, pictures fell from the wall, the decanter was knocked from the table. The sheriff released his grip on the girl, caught a chair for support. She was slammed against the wall. Both were wide-eyed with shock.

Johnny Liddell crossed the lawn on a run, skirted the fish pond and reached the French doors. He put his shoulder to them, heard the flimsy lock smash as he threw his weight.

Regan stood slack-jawed at the intrusion, his reflexes were slowed down by the shock. His hand streaked for the gun in the holster over the back of the chair. It froze with his fingertips touching the butt of his .38 at the sight of Liddell's .45 aimed at a spot inches above his belt buckle. He seemed to be having difficulty dragging his eye away from the yawning muzzle of the .45.

The blonde was the first to recover. She stared at Liddell wide-eyed. "You sure take a girl up on an invitation," she marveled. Her lips were parted, gleaming and wet; her eyes half veiled by artificially-tinted lids. The red gown gaped in front where Regan had pulled it away, revealing the white strips on her breasts and thighs usually covered by her bikini, contrasting with the nut-brown color of the rest of her body. She shook her head again. "Was it you set off that explosion?"

Liddell kept his eyes on Regan. "Your friend here might know something about that."

Regan's piglike eyes glared hatred at Liddell. "You better have a good reason for being here, mister."

"I have. I thought you'd like to know your little plan backfired."

The sheriff kept his eyes on the muzzle of the gun. "I'm getting awful tired of you. If you were smart, peeper——"

"What about that explosion?" the blonde demanded. "How would he know anything about it? He liked to drop dead he was so scared."

Liddell consulted his watch. "It's exactly 2:10, just about the time the Los Angeles plane that left here at 11:30 would be crossing the high point of the Rockies."

Regan continued to glare, didn't open his mouth.

The girl looked from Liddell to Regan and back. "So what's that got to do with an explosion around here?"

"It wasn't supposed to be around here. It was supposed to be on that plane," Liddell told her grimly. "I was supposed to be carrying a million in bills to a shakedown artist. Only the valise passed through a few hands before it reached me. When it finally did it carried a bomb instead of the money."

The blonde looked at the sheriff with distaste. "You knew about that, Regan? A plane full of people blown up just to get one man?"

"He's crazy."

Liddell kicked the doors shut behind him. "Sure. It's my imagination. So was that blast. I buried that suitcase a couple of miles from here. You heard it. You know what that would have done to a plane?"

"I won't forget this, shamus."

Liddell grinned at him glumly. "I'll bet you won't. Nei-

162

ther will the guy who substituted the bomb for the money." He waved Regan away from the chair holding his holster, tugged the .38 out and tossed it across the room. "Not a bad idea, at that. Everyone figures the million got blown up with the ship. Nobody looks for the hijacker. Too bad it didn't work, Regan."

"Well, why don't you say something, Regan?" the blonde sneered. "You can slap women and drunks around, why don't you take the gun away from him and make him eat it? You're forever telling me how tough you are. Now let's see you prove it."

"You shut up." He swung on Liddell. "If you think you're throwing a scare into me—"

"We know you're not scared, Sheriff," the blonde taunted. "Your knees are keeping time to music, not knocking."

The sheriff turned to glare at her. "I'm not forgetting this, either, Maisie. There'll be another time and another place."

"That's twice you bragged about your memory, Sheriff," Liddell told him. "That's good. Because I've got some questions I need answers to."

"I don't answer questions for a peeper," the sheriff spat. "I gave you all the breaks. Now, I'm going to stamp you so flat—"

"Sure. You gave me all the breaks. Including leaving a dead man in my room with my gun there. But then, I wouldn't mind, would I? I'd be on that plane, blown to bits. So you could write the case off."

Regan scowled. "What dead man?"

Liddell grinned at him. "It didn't work. They sent the maid to check my linen, but I'd already cleaned up by the time she got there."

The sheriff swore, charged at Liddell. Johnny side-stepped the lunge, laid the flat of his gun barrel along the side of the sheriff's head, knocked him to his knees.

"If you've got any idea you're not going to tell me what I want to know, you're crazy. You're going to tell me—" He leaned down over the prostrate man. "Or I'll leave you as toothless as the day you were born." He stuck the barrel of the .45 under the sheriff's nose. "Who killed Fat Mike?"

A thin film of perspiration formed on the sheriff's forehead. "He committed suicide," Regan said sullenly, glared at Liddell, then dropped his eyes.

Liddell grabbed a handful of the sheriff's hair, made his eyes meet his. "It was murder. And I've got the pictures to prove it." He grinned at the expression on the sheriff's face. "There were two sets. I let you get one. The state police are getting the other."

Regan stared at him for a moment, wiped the perspiration off his upper lip with the side of his hand. "I don't believe it."

"Then you better start trying to believe it, pal. The killer is going to be awful upset with you for snafuing the whole deal. He might even have it figured out that with everything going wrong and you being the only one who knows who he is—" Liddell shrugged. "He strikes me as a real neat soul. Doesn't like to leave loose ends lying around. And, brother, you're the loose end to end all loose ends." He grinned at the beaded perspiration glistening on the white-haired man's jowls. "Twice he gave you orders to get rid of me. Twice you blew it. How patient can he get?"

The sheriff stayed on his hands and knees, shook his head to clear it.

"Who gave him orders?" the blonde wanted to know.

"That's one of the things I came here for him to tell me." He reached down, caught the sheriff's shoulder,

164

pulled him up and shoved him into a chair. "He'll tell me. It may take time, but—"

Somewhere there was a screeching of brakes, the sound of a car door opening and slamming. Liddell swung his gun to cover the girl.

She shook her head. "I'm neutral. The more I hear of this the less I like it."

A door some place in the front of the house slammed open.

"Regan?" a voice bellowed. "Regan, where are you? All hell's broken loose and—" Liddell could hear the man stumbling against furniture in the darkened rooms. For a moment, he took his attention away from the man in the chair.

"Get out of here, you fool!" Regan bellowed. "Liddell's in here with a—"

The gun barrel described an arc, caught the sheriff on the side of the head, sent him sprawling out of his chair.

Liddell didn't wait. He sprinted for the door leading to the front of the house. For a moment, he was silhouetted against the lights behind him. A gun barked in the darkness, spitting orange flame. The slugs chewed chunks out of the door frame alongside Johnny. He dived for the floor.

He could hear the man running for the door, as it slammed behind him. Liddell wasted precious time feeling his way through the darkened room in the direction of the front of the house. He pulled open the door, stepped back out of range. There was no fire from outside.

Johnny rushed out the door, gun in hand. He walked onto the apron of the double garage, stood looking around. Suddenly he saw a big sedan, its lights out, heading for him.

Liddell yelled for the driver to halt, realized almost too late that instead of swinging around the circular driveway and heading for the highway, the driver was deliberately gunning the car at him. He heard the roar of the motor, the lights suddenly flashed on pinning him against the garage door. The big car, like a thing alive, was reaching for him.

The driver's face was an unrecognizable white blur in the interior of the car. Liddell's yell was drowned out by the roar of the big motor.

He raised his .45, started squeezing the trigger. The windshield fell to pieces around the driver's face as the big car continued to hurtle forward. Liddell felt trapped, rooted to the ground in its path. He kept squeezing the trigger. Suddenly, the big car seemed to go out of control, veered to the left as Liddell jumped to the right. Its fender brushed Liddell as it roared past, splintered the garage door and came to a shuddering, rending stop against the far brick wall of the garage.

Liddell wiped his streaming face, started toward the car.

"That's far enough, peeper," a harsh voice stopped him. He turned to see Sheriff Regan standing in the doorway of the house, his .38 in his hand. A dark trickle ran from his hair line, dripped from the point of his chin.

"I saw the whole thing. And it was cold-blooded murder." He stepped out of the doorway onto the driveway. "And since now you're trying to shoot it out with me—" His finger whitened on the trigger.

Liddell had a flash of the blonde stepping out of the door behind the sheriff. She raised a small wooden stool, shattered it over Regan's head. The sheriff staggered forward, his gun stuttering, the slugs digging trenches at Liddell's feet. Regan went down to his knees, sprawled out face down on the driveway.

166

"You all right?" the blonde called to Liddell.

He tried for a grin, almost made it. "I've been better," he conceded. He walked over to Regan, kicked the gun out of his hand onto the lawn. Then he walked over to the wrecked car.

Smoke was rising in a twisting spiral from under the dashboard. Inside, a man lay twisted, broken across the wheel.

"Should I call for an ambulance?" Maisie wanted to know.

Liddell leaned in, studied the open eyes staring sightlessly at the floor, the snapped off portion of the steering column that had entered below the breast bone, protruding like some obscene horn.

"Never mind an ambulance. This one's dead." He shook his head at the dead man. "If you'd had any sense, you would have stayed on that stretcher the first time. This is qualifying the hard way."

"Do you know him?" the blonde quavered from behind him.

"We have a nodding acquaintance." Liddell pulled his head out of the wrecked car, straightened up. "He worked for your boy friend—"

The blonde stared timorously into the car, shook her head. "He wasn't one of Regan's boys. Linehan and Breck, they do his dirty work. I never saw this one."

"So he worked for him indirectly, on loan. This character tried to kill me a couple of nights ago, spent the night in the morgue on a dead wagon for his trouble. He was on his way out to tell Regan their plans to plant Carl Jensen's body on me went haywire too."

Maisie turned toward the unconscious man in the driveway. "What about him?"

Liddell considered. "I guess we'll just have to wait until he wakes up and can answer a few questions."

"You really think he knows who did the killings?"

Liddell nodded his head. "It figures."

"Gee, that's like having a due bill on Fort Knox. A guy knowing the killer could put him in the hot seat just by spilling. That's really having a free pass."

"A free pass to the morgue sometimes. This killer wants something so bad he's killed twice to get it. One more kill to cover up won't bother him."

The blonde suddenly seemed to realize the flimsiness of her gown. She shivered and pulled it closer around her.

"Suppose he thinks Regan told me what he knows?"

Liddell shook his head. "What a waste of good material that would be." He walked over to where the sheriff lay on his face, turned him over. Regan was breathing heavily, gargling, sounding almost as if he were snoring. Liddell lit a match, lifted the unconscious man's eyelid, passed the match back and forward in front of the eye.

Finally he blew out the match, stood up. "You really handed him a clout."

"He's not dead?"

"He's not dead. But for all the good he's going to do me he might as well be. It could be hours, maybe days before he can answer any questions. And answers are what I need right now."

The blonde shook her head. "I'm sorry. I never have been able to do anything right."

Liddell grinned at her, patted her arm. "Don't take it so big. If you hadn't clouted him, I still wouldn't be in any position to get those answers. Not unless he learned how to use a ouija board."

"What are we going to do?"

Liddell looked down at the unconscious man, shrugged. "We'd better get him to a hospital, for one thing." He looked from Regan to the smashed car.

168

"What am I going to say? How can I explain what happened?"

Liddell reached down, caught Regan by the collar, dragged him to the car. He dumped him alongside the sprung door across from the driver.

"Simple. You heard this car come tearing into the driveway. There was a crash. Maybe the driver lost control when that explosion came." He pursed his lips. "You ran out, found the car rammed into the side of the garage. The driver you couldn't do anything for. The sheriff got thrown out of the car. You tried to make him comfortable and called an ambulance." He studied the girl's expression. "Make sense?"

Maisie bit on her lower lip. "And you? Where will you be?"

"Looking for some place else to get those answers. Think you can handle it without me?"

"And if Regan comes to before the ambulance gets here?"

Liddell considered, grinned glumly. "Tap him on the head again. It would be a waste of the taxpayers' money to get the ambulance all the way out here for nothing."

NINETEEN

The highway was still filled with emergency vehicles on their way to the scene of the explosion when Johnny Liddell reached his car in the shadow of the big tree. Other cars careened by, filled with morbid curiosity seekers who were trading in the excitement of the gaming tables for the excitement of possible catastrophe. In the distance there was the wail of a siren as ambulances were rushed to the scene from both the airport and the city itself.

As soon as the vehicles had passed, Liddell rolled his car back out onto the highway, headed in the opposite direction, back toward the Strip. When he passed the entrance to Maisie's driveway, he could barely make out the bulk of the big car telescoped against the garage wall.

It was 3:08 when he wheeled the car up the Strip toward the Music Hall. In about twenty minutes the passengers on the Las Palmas to Los Angeles flight would be debarking at the Municipal Airport in L.A., happily unaware that they had never been intended to make it.

Liddell parked his car in the Music Hall back lot, headed for Lee Loomis's bungalow. He shouldered his way through the clotted groups that filled the porte-

170

cochere and parking area propounding theories for the cause of the explosion that ranged from flying saucers to a misdirected missile from the Flats. They were all too engrossed in the current excitement for anyone to pay him any attention. He circled to the pool area, headed up the slight incline to Bungalow B.

Lee Loomis opened the door a few inches in response to his knock. Her eyes widened when she recognized Liddell. "Johnny, I thought—"

"I know. You thought I was on the Los Angeles flight." He pushed the door open, walked in.

The redhead closed it behind him, leaned against it. She was wearing the same nile-green dressing gown she had on when he first came to the bungalow. It was still doing the same wonderful job of showcasing her figure.

"What happened?" she asked.

"I got a hunch and rode it. I decided not to take that flight. Which was pretty lucky for the rest of the passengers. There was a bomb in that suitcase."

The redhead tried to swallow her fist. "A bomb!" She stared for a minute. "Is that what that explosion was—?"

Liddell nodded. "I took it out on the desert and buried it. I figured that if it was a bomb, it would be timed to go off just when the plane was over the mountains." He grinned glumly. "It was right on the dot." He walked over to help himself to a cigarette from a pack on the coffee table.

"But all those other people. People who never hurt anybody." She studied his face. "But how could you guess there was a bomb in there?"

Liddell took a deep drag, exhaled twin streams from his nostrils. "It figured. The shake artist is right here in town. He never intended to let that money get out of town. So he pulled a switch, held onto the money and

171

tried to get rid of two birds with one stone. And he had me figured for feathers."

"I told you, Johnny," the redhead moaned. "I told you they think nothing of murder." She caught him by the arm. "Let's get out of here. Let them kill each other off. It's none of our business."

Liddell laughed humorlessly. "That's what you think. There's a dead man in my bungalow. Carl Jensen. He's wearing bullets that came from my gun for shirt studs. That makes it my business." He took another drag on the cigarette, stubbed it out. "I've got to deliver the real killer or take a chance on taking the fall myself."

Lee Loomis stared at him. "If the bullets came from your gun—"

Liddell shook his head. "I didn't kill him. Sheriff Regan's boy took my gun when he shook down my room. They wanted to get rid of Jensen without any heat. So they figured I wouldn't mind if they used my facilities. After all by the time it was discovered they expected there wouldn't be enough of me left to pick up with a shovel."

"Do you think you can make the sheriff talk?"

"Nobody can in his present condition," Liddell grunted. "He's got a cracked skull and the guy who pulled the trigger is on his way to make a gin partner for Jensen in the morgue. But they're not the ones I want. I want the guy who ordered the trigger pulled."

"Johnny, I'm scared. How can you find him if everybody who could finger him is either dead or unable to talk?"

"I know who he is. I've known for quite a while. But I can't prove it. And unless I can he'll be taking off with that million dollars, leaving me holding the bag. And this time it'll go off in my face!" He peered at the redhead, studied her expression. "You willing to help me?"

The girl chewed on her lower lip. "I'll do anything I can."

Liddell nodded. "That's good enough." He dropped onto the couch, patted the pillow next to him, waited until she sank down alongside him. "There may be a little risk attached, but I'll do everything I can to cover your play. Still willing?"

Lee Loomis nodded slowly. "If you think it will help."

"It's a long shot," Liddell conceded. "But it's my only chance to walk away from this clean."

"Tell me what to do."

"I want you to call Marty Sommers, Benny Lewine, Al Rossi and Eddie Morrow. Tell them that the real reason Fat Mike sent for me was because he didn't trust Whitey—"

"But that's not true."

Liddell bobbed his head patiently. "I know it. You know it. And one other man will know it. The killer. That's where the risk will come in." He watched her expression, saw the color drain slightly from her face. "You'll tell them one other thing."

"Yes?"

"Tonight a valise came for Liddell. You happened to be out front when it arrived. Whitey took it, then walked with it to his office, came out with one that looked like it. You think he switched valises." He grinned at the strained expression on her face. "Think you can swing it?"

The redhead licked at her lips. "I can try."

Al Rossi's office in the Oasis was a combination of den and office. Its knotty pine paneling featured autographed pictures of the top talent that had headlined its shows, the floor was covered with a colorful Indian rug. Comfortable looking chairs were scattered around the room, Rossi's desk was placed so he commanded a full view of the room.

He hung up the telephone, swore loud and volubly. Then he tugged open the top drawer of his desk, took out a .45, checked its magazine. He stuck the gun in his waistband, got up and started for the door. With his hand on the doorknob, he stopped, reconsidered.

He walked back to the desk, picked up the telephone. "Get me Marty Sommers at the Las Palmas Arms," he growled. He drummed on the edge of the desk with spatulate fingers.

The resonant voice of Sommers came through the instrument. "Sommers."

"This is Rossi. You get a call from Fat Mike's broad?"

There was a worried note in Sommers's voice. "A few minutes ago."

"What are you going to do about it?"

Sommers hesitated. "What can we do?"

"What do you mean, what can we do? Whitey's been behind this shake. That shamus took a bagful of telephone books or old newspapers wherever he went. So he gets word to leave it some place. But nobody ever picks it up because Whitey already has the dough. Me, I'm not standing still for it."

"The girl could be wrong."

"Sure, she could," Rossi said. "But it makes more sense if she's right. The shake artist never has to show to pick up his dough. He has it all the time. I say we—"

The worried note was more pronounced in Sommers's voice. "We agreed to handle this together, Tony. No one of us is to take anything into his own hands."

"Okay, counselor, we do it your way. You have the broad and the rest of the boys in the penthouse in half an hour. I'll deliver Whitey."

"But—"

174

"In a half an hour. Or I do it my way."

. There was an uneasy pause at the other end of the phone. "Okay, Rossi," Sommers capitulated. "I'll have the girl here. You deliver Whitey."

"It'll be a pleasure." Rossi dropped the receiver back on its hook, glared at it. He reached down into his bottom drawer, brought out a bottle, poured himself a drink.

Whitey Sells stood at the long buffet table in the rear of the Music Hall, watched with satisfaction as the guests lined up, piled their plates high with all varieties of hors d'oeuvres. He was feeling at particular peace with the world. Official word had finally come through that the boys in Chicago had approved of him as Fat Mike's successor. On top of that, tonight's play was one of the heaviest he could remember.

He had had a couple of uneasy minutes earlier. A big Hollywood figure, noted for his belligerence when he'd had a few drinks, had gotten off on a run at one of the craps tables. He insisted on having the house limit removed, showed signs of creating a disturbance. Whitey had finally given the okay to take off the limits. At one point the player was into the house for almost twenty thousand but the vigarish soon went to work for the house and the Hollywood star was now sleeping it off in one of the bungalows, eighteen thousand dollars lighter in the wallet.

Whitey looked around the place, made mental notes on the changes he intended to make. Very few of his predecessor's policies appealed to him. One of the few reminders of Fat Mike he intended to keep around was the redhead currently headlining the show. But before he could do that, he had to do something about the shamus.

He was lost in reverie when one of the deputies walked

over. "Al Rossi of the Oasis is outside. Wants to see you, Whitey."

Whitey glared at him. "Mr. Sells. I'm operating the Music Hall as of now. The Whitey bit is out."

The deputy shrugged. "Okay, Mr. Sells. Rossi still wants to see you."

"Why doesn't he come in?"

"Says he don't have time. The big operators are having an important meeting. He dropped by to pick you up."

A slow, pleased smile split Whitey's face. "Word must be out already." He took a last look around the casino, satisfied himself that everything was running smoothly. "Okay. If anyone wants me, I'll be at Marty Sommers's penthouse at the Las Palmas Arms."

The deputy touched his fingers to the peak of his cap in a salute. He stepped back as Whitey pushed past him, watched him shoulder his way to the door.

On the way Whitey took notice of the stickmen on the craps layout, the dealers on 21. There'd be a lot of changes, he decided. Fat Mike had let things get too sloppy.

Outside the building he stood for a moment on the porte-cochere, let the breeze off the desert counteract the effects of too much time spent in the air-conditioned building. He looked around, spotted Rossi's Imperial pulled up on the far side of the driveway. He grimaced, made a note to tell the parking attendants that no one gets special parking privileges at the Music Hall. He crossed over to where it stood, motor humming, tugged open the door across from the driver.

Rossi was sitting behind the wheel. He waited until Whitey had stuck his head in. He had the .45 up, its muzzle inches from Whitey's face. "Get in."

Whitey hesitated a minute, decided he couldn't outrun a slug and no amount of deputies would do him any good with a hole in his head. He obeyed with alacrity, slipped in alongside Rossi.

"What is this?"

Rossi scowled at him. "Behave and you'll find out. Try anything fancy and you'll never know." He held the .45 in his left hand; its muzzle aimed at the man opposite. "Get over as far against the door as you can. Move one finger while I'm driving and I'll put a hole in you big enough to drive a Mack truck through."

Whitey licked at his lips, squeezed back against the door. Rossi shoved the car into drive, started rolling slowly toward the highway.

Lee Loomis sat on the couch in Bungalow B, chewed nervously on the cuticle of her thumb. It was almost half an hour since she had finished making the calls Liddell had laid out for her. She watched him going through the motions of making drinks at the portable bar at the far side of the room.

"Suppose the killer doesn't bite?" she wanted to know. "Suppose one of the boys just goes haywire and kills Whitey. It'd be on our conscience."

Liddell turned, brought two drinks from the bar, handed one to the girl. He dropped down onto the couch beside her. "Don't worry. The killer is plenty confused by now. The news of the plane being missing should have been on the air. Maybe he's already checked the airlines and found out that it landed safely." He sipped at his drink, grinned. "So now it makes sense that maybe Whitey did switch the valise. Maybe I delivered a phony and the one that was supposed to blow up the plane was buried by Whitey." He shook his head. "He's got to know. If that's what happened, Whitey can prove the original delivery was a phony—"

The telephone jangled on the coffee table. The redhead looked from the instrument to Liddell.

"Answer it."

Lee Loomis took a deep swallow from her glass, picked up the phone. "Yes?"

"Lee, this is Marty Sommers. I'm sorry to bother you."

"That's all right."

The counselor seemed to be groping for words. "One of the boys, Al Rossi, wants to hold a meet. He wants you to make your accusation to Whitey to his face—"

"I couldn't do that," the redhead gasped. "Please, Mr. Sommers, I was only trying to do you all a favor. I didn't think—"

"There's no danger, Lee. Maybe Whitey can explain it all away. Anyhow you'll be protected either way."

The redhead's eyes beseeched Liddell, he nodded for her to agree.

"But if I could just—"

A hard note crept into the attorney's voice. "I don't like this any more than you do, Lee. It's a tough spot for all of us. But I think it'll be best for all of us to get this settled one way or another."

Lee Loomis's voice quavered. "If you think so—"

"I'll have my car pick you up."

The redhead wagged her head. "No, don't bother. I'll have one of the deputies drive me over. It—It'll save time that way."

"However you want it," the counselor told her. "Just be here."

The redhead dropped the receiver on its hook, stared at Liddell. "What'll I do? They want me to face Whitey and accuse him of switching the valises."

"I'll be there backing your play."

178

The redhead drained her glass, got up, walked to the bar and refilled her glass. She drained it in a swallow. "I hope you know what you're doing."

Liddell smiled grimly. "I hope you get your hope."

TWENTY

Whitey Sells stood in the living room of Marty Sommers's penthouse, his eyes moving angrily from face to face. "What's the idea, Sommers?"

The counselor shrugged. "We're going to have a meeting. We thought you might like to sit in."

"That the way you hand out invites? A .45 under my nose?"

Sommers managed to look hurt. "We asked Al to make sure you didn't miss it. You tell Al to bring somebody, he only knows one way."

Whitey turned, glared at the man in the silk suit. "You got it in your head I'm some small-time punk you can push around, forget it. The boys up north just okayed me for the Music Hall. They're not going to like it if—"

"We got shaken for a cool million tonight," Rossi told him in a hard, flat tone. "We think you know something about it. And friends or no friends up north, if you were mixed up in it you're not walking out of here."

Whitey's jaw sagged, he looked around for some indication he was being needled as a new member of the

180

combine. "You been using a needle? I don't know nothing about any shakedown."

"We got somebody who says you do."

"Who?" An angry flush darkened Whitey's normal pallor. "You show him to me. Let him tell me that to my face."

"That's just what we're going to do," Marty Sommers told him. "If there's a mistake, we'll apologize." He indicated the bar by the window. "It may take a few minutes. Why don't we all relax and have a drink while we're waiting?"

Rossi shook his head, stood glaring at Whitey Sells. Benny Lewine walked over, started pouring some scotch into each of four glasses.

The door to the lobby of the Las Palmas Arms exploded open, Johnny Liddell stumbled in. Before he could get his balance, Tommy Thompson, the deputy from the Music Hall caught him by the arm, propelled him to the elevator bank. Lee Loomis followed sedately.

At the elevator, Farmer, Sommers's driver got up from his chair, looked around, satisfied himself the entrance hadn't created too much of a disturbance. "What's the idea, friend?" he asked placidly.

Tommy pushed Liddell toward the door of the elevator. "Your boss called the Music Hall. Said the boys wanted to see this character, and they didn't care what condition he was in when he got here."

The man in the rumpled suit flicked Liddell's jacket open, satisfied himself the shoulder holster was empty. "They told me the girl would be coming. Nobody said anything about him." A perplexed frown furrowed his forehead. "I'm not supposed to take anyone up without the boss okays it." He looked Liddell over with a jaundiced expression. "I know he's been here before—" He shook his head uncertainly. "I better let the boss know he's on his way up."

He started around Liddell, found the deputy blocking his way. The deputy's gun was pointed at Farmer's midsection.

He dropped his eyes from Tommy's face to the gun. "What's the idea?"

"Why stand on ceremony?" Tommy grunted. "Let's take him up."

Farmer's eyes traversed the lobby wildly, found no one to help. His eyes dropped again to the gun in his midsection, saw the deputy's finger whiten on the trigger. He stepped into the elevator, Liddell followed him in.

"Face the back," Johnny told him. The man in the rumpled suit complied.

The redhead walked into the cage, followed by Tommy.

Liddell reached around the guard, fanned him expertly, came up with a .38, handed it to Thompson.

"I'll get out at the penthouse with Lee. You can handle him, can't you?"

Thompson grinned glumly, nodded. He brought the barrel of the .45 down on the guard's head. Farmer crumpled to the floor, a tangle of arms and legs. "Might as well take him out of play. We may be in a hurry on our way out. Right?"

Liddell shrugged. "Could be. I'll ring three short ones. That'll mean come running."

Tommy nodded. "I'll be there."

At the penthouse floor, Liddell and the redhead got off. They waited until the cage had started down. Then Liddell flattened himself against the wall at the end of the corridor, Lee Loomis stepped up to the door. She

182

looked down to Liddell, he held the tip of his index finger to the ball of his thumb, winked.

She turned, knocked at the door.

Inside Marty Sommers set his half-finished scotch down on the coffee table, walked to the door, opened it. Lee Loomis walked in.

"Hello, Lee. Thanks for coming."

The redhead walked through the small dark vestibule into the living room. Her eyes jumped from face to face in the room, came to rest on Whitey Sells.

"What's she doing here?" Whitey growled.

"You'll find out." Rossi told him. He turned back to the redhead. "Suppose you tell him what you told us over the phone earlier."

The redhead walked across the room to the picture window, every eye in the room followed her.

"If she said I knew anything about any shake, she's a liar," Whitey roared.

"Shut up and let her speak her piece," Rossi growled.

Lee licked at her lips. "Mike Klein was afraid of Whitey. He thought Whitey murdered Adams. That's why he sent for Liddell."

Whitey stared at her, his eyes widening until the irises were rimmed with white. "You're lying." He started for her, Rossi caught him by the collar, pulled him back.

"Go on."

"I called Mike from the airport when I arrived with Liddell. He said he was going to have Whitey drive him to—"

Whitey shook off Rossi's hand, made a lunge for the girl. Rossi brought up his foot, Whitey fielded the kick with his groin, collapsed in a heap.

"I shouldn't have let that elevator jockey of yours collect my gun," Rossi stood over the fallen man. "I'd give it to him right here."

On the floor, Whitey was twisting and squirming, his knees up under his chin, unable to cry out from the pain that tore at him. Rossi kicked him under the ribs, brought up his foot to stomp him.

"Hold it," Lewine grunted. "Anything happens to him, it shouldn't be here." He walked over, helped Whitey to his feet, supported him to the couch. Whitey moaned, turned his face to the back of the couch, brought his knees up to protect his mid-section.

Sommers wasted an incurious glance on the man on the couch. "Now about the valise."

The redhead pulled her knuckle from between her teeth, struggled for composure. Most of her color had drained from her face. She fought a losing battle to keep her eyes off the man on the couch. "I saw a man leave it with Whitey. He took it to his office. I waited because I wanted to talk to him. It was almost ten minutes before he came out and checked it at the checkroom. I recognized it later when Liddell told me there was a million dollars in it."

Eddie Morrow had the tic under his eyes again. "Sounds like the old switch, all right." He ran the heel of his hand along his jaw. "He's got to be the shake artist or we would have heard from the real one by now." He looked around for confirmation. "Because if he pulled a switch just to get the dough and the real one thought we were trying to double-cross him—" His voice quavered at the prospect.

"Whitey was behind it, all right," Rossi scowled. "Give me ten minutes with him alone, I'll find out where he has it stashed away. The Bug had a way of asking questions so a guy begged to spill everything he knew."

"Just a minute," Sommers put in. "So far, we're all clean in this town. There's not a rap they can pin on us and I vote we keep it that way."

184

"How about our dough?" Lewine wanted to know.

"I want it back as much as you do," Sommers agreed. "But nothing happens to him in my place. And I want no part of a hit."

Rossi looked to the other men in the room. "How about it? Do we stand still for a shake? Or do we serve notice right now on any other petty-larceny chiseler who might be getting ideas about us?"

The others avoided his eyes.

He hit his chest with the side of his hand. "Well, I'm not standing still for it."

Marty Sommers swabbed at his jowls with a balled handkerchief. "Let's put it to a vote, Rossi."

"Okay. I move we make an example of this creep." Rossi looked to Lewine. "You, Benny?"

The ex-pug considered a moment, nodded his head hesitantly. "I guess they need an example. The young punks!"

Rossi turned to Morrow. "You?"

Morrow kept his eyes caroming around the room to avoid Marty Sommers's gaze. He nodded.

Rossi turned back to the counselor. "It's three to one. Want to make it unanimous?"

Sommers shook his head. "Majority rules. But I'll tell you this. I kept my nose clean on the Big One in all my years in Chicago. I'm not getting mixed up in a kill down here."

No one heard the faint click as Liddell worked the lock from the hallway with a piece of celluloid. He slipped in the door, flattened against the wall in the darkened vestibule.

"You're not with us, you're against us," Rossi was telling Sommers in a hard, flat voice.

Sommers nodded. "I know how you feel. I'll be getting out of Las Palmas as soon as I can clean things up. As

185

long as you're convinced that Whitey killed Adams and Mike and—"

Liddell stepped into the room. "But he didn't."

Unconsciously, Rossi's hand raced for his holster, he cursed under his breath when his fingers encountered the empty hammock. "How'd you get here?"

"The same way you did. On the elevator."

The redhead ran over to Liddell, caught his arm. "Nobody ever looked so good to me, Johnny. I—I thought they were going to kill him."

Sommers frowned at Liddell. "I can't imagine why you're here, Liddell. You were supposed to make that payoff. Could it be that you and Whitey—?"

"Whitey had no part of it, Sommers," Liddell told him. "You should know that. The whole idea was yours."

Lewine looked from Liddell to the counselor and back. "You're crazy. He got clipped for two-fifty just like the rest of us."

"Wouldn't you put up two-fifty to get a million?" Liddell didn't take his eyes off the counselor.

"I suppose you have some basis for this ridiculous accusation?" Sommers growled.

"I've known it for quite a while. Proving it took time." Liddell turned to Rossi. "You ever speak to this shake artist? Or Lewine or Morrow?" He shook his head. "Just Sommers."

Rossi managed to look thoughtful.

"You're trying to cover up the fact that you bungled the payoff," Sommers told him. "Of course I spoke to the extortionist, but—"

Liddell ignored the interruption. "The funny thing is that the shakedown was practically an afterthought. You had another reason for killing Adams and Klein. The first letter was sent just to make it look like a shake artist was at work. But the boys ran so scared you figured nothing should go to waste so you went ahead with the shake."

"And this other reason?"

"Adams and Fat Mike were getting out of Las Palmas. They were set to open a big operation in Tia Juana. They kept the secret." He grinned glumly at Sommers. "From everybody except their legal adviser. When he saw how big the operation really was, he decided to cut himself in. And them out."

Some of the doubt was draining from Lewine's eyes. The old-time hard look was in its place. "And the first letter was a cover-up?"

Liddell nodded. "But a million just for the taking is a little too tough to pass up. When I came on the scene, the counselor decided I might get too curious—"

"You're forgetting something. I was the one who stopped the sheriff from running you out of town."

"What you were afraid of was that somebody would get proof to Fat Mike's pals he was murdered. When the sheriff told you he got my pictures from the post office, you decided running me out of town wasn't enough. You decided to fix me permanently. That's why you insisted that I make the payoff."

The counselor's eyes were hopping around the room, gauging the reactions on the other faces. "You're crazy. The sheriff will tell you—"

"Don't count on Regan. He's where he'll be singing like a stage-struck canary in a birdseed factory. Now that you can't deliver on making him the casino boss in the Tia Juana set-up—"

. Sommers moved swiftly. His hand darted under his left lapel, came up with a .45. "I don't know how you managed to get back here, Liddell. But as long as you did, I guess this is where you'll have to stay. All of you."

Eddie Morrow was sweating profusely, the twitching under his eye more pronounced. "Give us a break, counselor. You got my two-fifty. Keep it, I don't want no part of it back. I won't put up a squawk."

"He couldn't take the chance," Rossi growled. "But the syndicate will reach him no matter where he goes. Go ahead, kill us, sucker. You're deader than any of us right now."

The redhead tightened her grip on Liddell's arm. "Do something, Johnny."

"He's done enough already," Sommers told her. "There isn't a gun in this room except the one I'm holding. Open his jacket."

The redhead flipped open the jacket. The holster hung under his arm, empty.

"So that explosion out near the airport was the valise, eh?" He eyed Liddell curiously. "How did you tumble?"

Liddell shrugged. "You start from a point. I started from the point that you were the shake artist. Therefore, there wouldn't be any money in that valise. You wouldn't let it out of your hands. You wanted me out of the way and you wanted no trace of the fact that the million stuck to your fingers." He shrugged again. "What would be neater than to put a bomb in it and do both at the same time?"

Sommers sighed. "It would have been so much simpler. In a month, maybe two, I could take over in Tia Juana. But you've spoiled all that." He looked to the couch where Whitey was groaning his way back to consciousness. "That was a smart move, having the girl tell that story of the switch. You fooled me. I actually thought Whitey did make the switch and bury the dynamite in the desert thinking it was the million."

"Why did you have Jensen killed?"

Sommers considered. "Same reason I wanted you out of the way. He was convinced Mike and Adams had been murdered. It would be very inconvenient if word of it got back to New York. So I arranged to eliminate him in your room with your gun." He sighed again. "All that careful planning gone for nothing." From the corner of his eye he saw the man on the couch struggle to get up.

Sommers swung as Whitey reached for a bottle that stood on the table next to the couch.

Liddell shoved the girl away from him, reached around to where he had the snub-nosed .38 stuck in the waistband in the back of his trousers. The .38 barked first.

Sommers's gun hand jerked, the .45 fell from his nerveless fingers. He grabbed his wrist, bent over it, rocked back and forth, crooning over the smashed fingers.

Rossi started for Sommers.

"Hold it," Liddell snapped. He covered the other with the .38.

Rossi bared his teeth. "So you are in it?"

Liddell shook his head. "A little unfinished business. Like I said there's a dead man in my closet with bullets from my gun in him. You all heard Sommers admit he had him killed."

"It wouldn't be admitted as testimony," Sommers snapped at him.

"A dying declaration is always admissible," Liddell reminded him. "And from the looks of your friends, unless you get up that money, that's what it's likely to be."

Rossi nodded grimly. "He'll get up the money."

"I'll bet," Liddell nodded. "How about the guy in my closet?"

Rossi looked to the other operators, they nodded. "It'll be our pleasure. You say the sheriff isn't available?"

"No, I don't think he'll be returning to the job, but

I've got a good replacement for him. I'll send the guy up to see you. His name's Thompson."

Whitey managed to get his feet on the floor, pulled himself to his feet. "He works for me," he protested weakly.

"We'll talk about it. First things first. First we find ways of getting our money back," Rossi kept his eyes on Sommers. "I nominate me a committee of one to handle that. Any objections?"

There were none.

Liddell started for the door. "By the way, Sommers was right about one thing. You don't have to dirty your hands with murder. When I get out of here, I'm mailing the pictures proving Fat Mike was murdered to his friends in New York."

Rossi nodded. "We'll leave enough of him for them."

Liddell led the redhead through the door into the hall, closed the door after them. He punched the elevator button three times. From some place close there was an agonized wail.

"What'll they do to him?"

Liddell shrugged. "Take back their money. Then they'll turn him loose and let him run." The elevator whooshed to a stop, the doors opened. "The syndicate will put a pencil mark around his name and he'll be a fair hit any place in the world. He won't live much longer this way, but it'll seem a lot longer. In the end, he couldn't be deader."

They stepped into the elevator, grinned down at the man in the rumpled suit who sat with his back against the wall, massaging the top of his head.

"Nothing personal, Farmer," Liddell assured him. He turned to the redhead, wondered if Muggsy would ap-

190

preciate it even a little if he interrupted her while she was at work. He decided, in deference to her feelings in the matter, to postpone seeing her until she got back to New York.

TO THE READER

If you enjoyed this book, you will be glad to know that there are many others just as well written, just as interesting, to be had in the Fiction House Press Library.

You will find the Fiction House Press Library online at

www.FictionHousePress.com

www.ingramcontent.com/pod-product-compliance
Lightning Source LLC
Chambersburg PA
CBHW020330260626
47156CB00004B/1466